BEST
GAY
EROTICA
2007

BEST
GAY
EROTICA
2007

Series Editor

RICHARD LABONTÉ

Selected and Introduced by

TIMOTHY J. LAMBERT

CLEIS
PRESS

Cleis Press Inc., P.O. Box 14697,
San Francisco, California 94114

Printed in the United States.
Cover design: Scott Idleman
Cover photograph: Celesta Danger
Text design: Frank Wiedemann
Cleis logo art: Juana Alicia
First Edition.
10 9 8 7 6 5 4 3 2 1

For Asa Dean Liles,
for our first fifteen years
for surviving his first Canadian winter

CONTENTS

ix Foreword • RICHARD LABONTÉ

xiii Introduction: Get Out of My House •
       TIMOTHY J. LAMBERT

  1 I Was JT LeRoy's Buttboy • SIMON SHEPPARD
 11 Coming to Grief • DALE CHASE
 23 Benediction • ALANA NOEL VOTH
 40 Sucksluts Anonymous • SCOTT D. POMFRET
 51 from *Push:* Williamsburg Swimming Pool •
       BLAIR MASTBAUM
 62 Damaged • DAVID MAY
 77 Remembered Men • SHANE ALLISON
 86 Riverboat Queens • DOMINIC SANTI
 93 The Welcome-Back Fuck • DALE LAZAROV
       AND DRUB
102 Hot Sales Guy • ALEX STRAND
117 The Lighthouse Keep: A Gothic Tale • JAY NEAL
130 Kurt • JONATHAN ASCHE
143 Saturday Punk • BOB CONDRON
151 from Bill in Exile • C. SCOTT SMITH
       AND WILLIAM MELOYD CULLUM
177 Disaster Relief • GREG HERREN
188 There's More to Kink Than Leather •
       CAT TAILOR

205 About the Authors
211 About the Editors

FOREWORD

Sex with an infamous and surprisingly butch
"author," the deep pain of a best friend turning his back on sex, sex in a roomful of cocksucking addicts, the rediscovery of sex.

Rough sex in the wake of a lover's death, hasty
sex with a boy in a swimming pool, fragmented
memories of sex with many, many men.

Sex sublimated into a drunken pillow fight,
sex with a ruff 'n' tuff ghost, crazy sex with an
imaginary man, satisfying sex with a married
man, a married man's wistful memories of sex
with his boyhood buddy.

Letters to and from prison about sex and life,
sex with a government official that's anything
but disastrous, surprising sex with a bar full of
drag queens, a graphic tale of fucking....

One thing *Best Gay Erotica* has never been:

a cookie-cutter anthology of themed porn short stories. This isn't a collection all about cowboys, though Dale Chase writes with wrenching emotion about one cowboy's lament; the theme isn't "my first time," though Alana Noel Voth writes with sad compassion about one adolescent's rebuffed longing; this isn't a collection about S/M, though Cat Tailor writes with jolly insight about one dominant top's humbling comeuppance; the theme isn't "sex with straight men," though... well, you get the idea. Something for everyone. That's the aim of this series.

Since 1996, guest judges—this year, novelist and editor Timothy J. Lambert, one-quarter of one best-selling writing team and one-half of another—have aimed to select a collection with depth, flair, and a certain perspective: that compelling, arousing storytelling and well-crafted, literate writing are quite comfy together between the covers of the same book.

I'll break with tradition here to single out—though every story is a Best, else why would it be here?—Simon Sheppard's completely believable account of being boned by JT LeRoy; it's a hilarious send-up of the queerest literary hoax ever, one of which we are, um, proud to have been a part. See *Best Gay Erotica 2002* and *Best of Best Gay Erotica 2*....

I'd also like to single out the comix included this year by Dale Lazarov, with illustrations by Drub. It's no simple thing to use words to craft a story that is involving, entertaining, and stimulating all at the same time. Year after year, the quality of the writers selected for this series energizes me. And when one of the finest tales is told without words—well, that's indeed a delight.

Thanks are always due: to Timothy J., of course, and to everyone who submitted work, whether chosen or not; to Cleis publishers Frédérique Delacoste and Felice Newman, and publicity director extraordinaire Diane Levinson; to the regulars in my life, Justin Chin and Kirk Read and Lawrence Schimel and Eddie Moreno; to newer friends: David Rimmer of After Stonewall Bookstore in Ottawa; Frank Kajfes and Bryan Wannop, the embodiment of hospitality, and honest men at last, after thirty years; and Jules Chamberlain, a fairy brother lover of good writing.

Richard Labonté
Perth/Calabogie, Ontario
August 2006

INTRODUCTION:
GET OUT OF MY HOUSE

I was a natural on skis, or so my instructor proudly told me. I could easily turn, snowplow, and maneuver gracefully down the trail, eventually leaving the class behind and exploring the mountain on my own with the instructor's blessing. I hopped on a lift, which carried me to greater heights, delighting at the view of the valley behind me as it dropped farther away. I hesitated briefly at the top of a steep intermediate trail, but then pushed off, flying swiftly on packed powder and instantly forgetting everything I'd previously learned. I tucked in to protect myself, anticipating slamming into a tree, another skier, or the lodge at the bottom of the slope, which was rapidly approaching as I gained momentum. I knew I should snowplow, turn, fall, do whatever I could to stop myself or slow down, but I was too frightened to do anything but steel myself for whatever and watch the world rush by in a maddening blur.

I must not have been in mortal peril, because my life didn't flash before my eyes. Which is unfortunate, because if it had, I would have seen that there would be many more instances where I'd impulsively jump off of metaphorical mountains without thinking of the consequences: not going to college and moving to New York City instead; experimenting with drugs; jumping from one horrible job to another; having bad relationships. I've always had two mottos: *I can do anything* and then later, when flying out of control down a metaphorical mountain: *Everything is going to be okay in the end.*

The first time I made love with a man was no different. He was almost too pretty to look at directly, so I'd furtively glance at his alabaster skin, full lips, and crystalline blue eyes while wondering why he allowed a know-nothing like me to fuck him. I plunged in, holding his feet over my head, and my thrusting escalated as we moved into a clumsy rhythm. It was over too quickly, but his kisses and appreciative murmuring seemed to indicate that I'd done something right. Just like on that first run down the ski slopes, I'd coasted to a safe stop, none the worse for wear and frightened for no apparent reason. Everything was okay in the end.

I could have been seriously injured during that first run on the mountain. I could have broken a leg, or worse, slammed into somebody else and broken someone else's leg, but I didn't let that fear stop me once I was at the bottom of the mountain and safely standing still. Instead, I went back up the lift and did it again, this time turning correctly and moving at a leisurely pace, enjoying the scenery.

Sex was a lot like skiing. Practice made perfect. It was better to slow down and enjoy the landscape of men that Manhattan had to offer. However, I still appreciated a dangerous quickie every now and then. It was exciting to fuck a total stranger in the open air of Central Park, knowing that the longer you took to come the greater the chance of being caught. Sometimes being caught was a good thing, like when another guy wanted to join in the fun. One of my favorite places to have sex was on the roof of my apartment building at night, surrounded by the lights of the city and thousands of windows of neighboring buildings. The thought that somebody could be watching always intensified my performance.

My favorite outdoor experience was on the very same mountain where I'd learned to ski. I was dating a wonderful man and had brought him to the homeland. The pressure of his meeting the family was intense, as was my yearning, which was due to complying with my parents' rather Victorian notion that the two of us should sleep in separate bedrooms. However, I got around that the next day when we took to the mountains to ski. I managed to get my guy alone by steering us to a lift that took us to a part of the mountain with new and partially developed trails, where I knew nobody liked to ski because of the icy terrain. As I'd predicted, there was no one there. At the top of the peak on the farthest side of the mountain, with the wind whipping around us, I pulled him to me and made my demands.

He laughed nervously, but I could tell he was intrigued with the idea. Before he could change his mind, my gloves were off and my hands were unzipping my pants, then his. The air was bracing, which worked to my advantage because it caused us to press our bodies against each other for warmth, for desire, for more.

As he sucked me off, I looked around at the beauty of our surroundings, and at this beautiful man who loved me. I could see the lodge far below us, looking like something I'd made as a child with my Lincoln Logs. I wondered if anybody from the ski patrol was inside, watching us through binoculars. I didn't care. Let them catch us, banish me forever from the mountain, or arrest us and cause my family even more shame. Both caution and sperm were thrown to the wind as my lover and I clung to each other and masturbated, ejaculating on the mountainside and claiming it as ours that day.

I haven't been to that mountain in quite some time. I haven't been much of anywhere, lately. Another writer sent me an email recently and part of his message said, "I just have to ask, how come you don't leave your house much? I've seen you make comments from time to time, but I always thought you were kidding."

My writing partner, Becky Cochrane, often jokes that I'm turning into "the gay J.D. Salinger" because I rarely leave the house. This isn't true for many reasons, among them: you know of J.D. Salinger. I'm not that famous a recluse. If W. Somerset Maugham was "in the very first row of the second-raters," then I'm in Standing Room Only. Although I don't have any statistics, I'm quite certain I'm not the only gay recluse, either. I'm willing to bet there are thousands of homosexuals wary of walking out their front door, lest they be severely beaten or called upon to smarten up their heterosexual neighbor's husband's attire.

I moved to Houston shortly before the Supreme Court agreed to hear the case of Lawrence v. Texas, which was an eye-opening experience. Perhaps because I was raised a Yankee, or because of my ignorance, it never occurred to me that two men could be arrested for having sex in the safety of their own home. Being a connoisseur of the ups and downs of sex out of doors, arrests such as George Michael's in 1993—entrapment or not—made perfect sense to me. The fact that sex out of doors is illegal is half the fun, I say.

However, being arrested inside your own home seemed barbaric to me, definitely not in keeping with a new century, and I was quite thrilled when the Supreme Court struck down the law. But what did it mean to me? It's not like I was having sex, indoors or out. I was hardly leaving my own yard. And why was that?

I could blame it on writing. As a writer of contemporary literature and romance, I can live vicariously through different characters and write about the sort of world in which I'd like to live, rather than reality, where people want to amend our Constitution to add discrimination, or look the other way while people are beaten senseless.

Reality is frightening sometimes, and often boring. Recently, at a party—which was at a neighbor's house, across the street, so I barely left the house, if you're wondering—I was talking with a man about why I don't date any longer. I lamented that people have changed; social niceties are no longer in style and everybody's only out for himself, it seems. The man with whom I was speaking—I'll refer to him as Bob, since that's his name—agreed with me then laughed when I said it had been years since I'd met anyone worth blowing, let alone carrying on a conversation with.

"I'll try not to take that personally," he said.

"You shouldn't," I agreed. "I was only trying out that line aloud to see if it would work for something I'm writing. You laughed, so it's in."

"Good," he said. "But if you don't mind my asking, how do you expect to meet anyone, much less blow him, if you don't leave the house?"

As clever as I like to believe that I am, I had no witty rejoinder for Bob. I thought about the stories I'd recently read for this anthology. I thought about skiing. I thought about my years in New York City. I thought about sex on a rooftop. Dorothy left Oz then promptly summed up everything into a lovely moral. Everything she needed was in her own backyard. Bully for her, but the bitch had too many morals. If it were me, I would've grabbed a ranch hand or two and headed directly for the hayloft.

"It's official," I stated. "I'm tired of fading to black."

I was recently asked—along with Becky—to speak on a panel at a gay literary festival about my experiences writing romance. (Okay, yes. I do leave the house on occasion. I told you I'm not the gay Salinger.) Somebody asked about writing sex scenes. Were they necessary? Did our readers expect them? Do sex scenes add to the story, or do they detract from the literary element of a gay romance novel?

I can't remember, word for word, our brilliant reply. But our fellow panelists, our moderator included, turned in shock as we confessed to our penchant for "fading to black." Fading to black is a term for building up to a sex scene, showing your characters undoing buttons, kissing, groping, and then cutting to them basking in the afterglow in the next chapter or paragraph. Fading to black gives readers an opportunity to get creative and decide for themselves what happened, to make up their own sex scene.

While this is fine and dandy for our books, I'm tired of living my life like a Timothy James Beck or a Cochrane Lambert character. I'm tired of imagining my own sex life. As George Michael said, "Let's go outside."

The majority of the stories in *Best Gay Erotica 2007* are about people who walk out the front door and have an adventure. I responded immediately to Blair Mastbaum's story, "Williamsburg Swimming Pool," which reminded me of my New York days, when a sexual invitation could arise in the most extraordinary of circumstances or locations. Or, sometimes, even the ordinary ones. Having grown up on the rocky and jagged coastline of Maine, I could intimately imagine myself in the role of the protagonist of Jay Neal's gothic tale. Next time I'm visiting the homeland, I'll make it a point to have my car break down near the closest lighthouse I can find.

My first foray into publishing centered on a female impersonator named Daniel, so I felt a certain fondness for the drag queens in "There's More to Kink Than Leather." I couldn't help but cheer them on as they turned the tables on poor Jason. He had it coming. So to speak. "Saturday Punk" made me want to fly to Dublin, find Larry, and offer myself to him posthaste. Or somebody like him. I suppose I could save money and drive around Houston picking up hitchhikers. At least I'd be out of the house.

But sometimes sex comes to your home when you least expect it, as I've learned in the past. Maybe someday I'll write a story about how I got my UPS cap. Until then, by all means skip ahead and read Greg Herren's "Disaster Relief," where sex is soothing, voracious, and timely.

While you're reading that, and the other deliciously sizzling stories in this tome, I'm going to get out of my house and look for adventure. There's no snow here, so maybe I'll go waterskiing. Or maybe I'll go to the park and try to lure some hot joggers off the beaten path. Better yet, maybe I'll hit the bookstore and pick up some of the previous volumes in this series, as well as a hot stud to read them to in bed.

Timothy J. Lambert
Houston
July 2006

I WAS JT LEROY'S BUTTBOY

Simon Sheppard

The voice on the phone was soft, almost feminine. "Simon?"

I knew who it was immediately. "Yeah," I said. "Hi, JT."

I'd first heard from JT LeRoy via email; he'd gotten in touch with me when our stories had been published next to each other—cheek by jowl, as t'were—in *Best of the Best Gay Erotica 2*. That had been something of a thrill for me, actually, seeing as how JT was the Hot New Thing on the San Francisco alternalit scene, a rising star who was hitting it big—Danielle Steel for the thinking queer. For half a decade, he'd blazed a trail across the Bay Area's literary firmament; his "preternaturally mature" (*Kirkus Reviews*) work had attracted the attention of such queer superstars as Gus

Van Sant, and his book *The Heart Is Deceitful Above All Things* had already been turned into a movie.

And now JT LeRoy was emailing me—me!—to tell me how much he liked my silly little tale about tricking with a diaperboy on meth, a piece that faded into insignificance, really, compared to his clearly autobiographical, "savagely authentic" (John Waters) story of a teenage hustler hired by a sadistic john. I was being honored by the attentions of an avant-garde legend-in-the-making, a wunderkind who wore a necklace of raccoon penis bones and wrote with the skill and daring of someone twice his age. A-fucking-mazing!

But then, I supposed he appreciated my stories of anomic, drugged-out hustlers and homeless kids, though they formed only part of my—oh, let's call it an *oeuvre*, shall we? What the hell...

"It's great to talk with you again."

"Same here. What can I do for you?" I knew that there probably would be *something* I could do for him: proofread a manuscript, help him out with a plot point, something. Granted, I wasn't as big a deal as many of his friends, folks like Dennis Cooper and that singer from Garbage. But I was always accessible, and I found it hard to say no. If part of that was just compassion, it was also due to the fact that I eroticized hard-luck hustler boys, boys like JT had been before he found the balm of writerly creativity, and...well, we all have mixed motives, don't we? Anyway, being literarily hit on by JT was still a lot more flattering than other events in what I with increasing despair thought of as "my career," things like the dismissive response of one publisher who, when I objected to my customary fee being cut in half, responded, "If you don't like it, I'd be happy to pull your story from the antho." Yeah, doing scutwork for JT LeRoy was massively better than that.

"Simon," said JT LeRoy in his high-pitched Southern drawl, "I'd like to meet you."

"For real?" I was amazed. JT was notoriously shy. He never read his own work in public, getting celebrities—increasingly, major-league ones—to stage readings instead. The few times he showed up in public, he appeared in disguise, a short boy in a hat, blond wig, and big sunglasses. If Greta Garbo had written stories about truck-stop whoring, she would have been JT LeRoy.

"For real. When can I come over?"

"Would you like me to come visit you instead? Or meet some neutral place, a coffee shop or something?"

"Your place. Say nine tomorrow night?"

I'd never entertained such a Famous Author at home before. Naturally, I was nervous as hell; now there would only be two degrees of separation between me and Courtney Love. There was no way I could remake my place overnight—it would remain a cluttered outpost of bohemia. But I rearranged my piles of books, making sure that if JT looked at them, he'd spot Foucault and Bataille, not Agatha Christie and Ellery Queen.

At last I relaxed and waited for the doorbell to ring.

It did, only thirty-three minutes late.

I'm on the top floor, so when I opened my apartment door, clomping footsteps echoed in the stairwell.

"Simon?"

I damn near fell over. I'd been expecting a shy, sexually ambiguous little alterna-boy, probably in a blond wig.

"Hi. I'm JT LeRoy."

There in my doorway stood a handsome, bearded, middle-

aged man, really tall—maybe six foot five—and dressed head
to toe in gleaming black leather. I was speechless, utterly
speechless. And—I admit it—turned on.

"Aren't you going to invite me in?"

My eyes drifted down to his basket, a big, blue denim bulge
framed by black chaps. Nice. "Sure, JT. Come in." And then I
had not one fucking idea of what to say next.

"Yeah," LeRoy or whoever said, "I know what you're thinking. Surprised, huh?"

I found words, sort of. "But...but...the person I spoke with
on the phone..."

The butch man in leather smiled. "What about him?" His
voice had suddenly gone up an octave and gained a Southern
accent.

"Jesus," I said. "Jesus, Jesus, Jesus." The literary find of the
decade was, apparently, the literary hoax of the new millen-
nium...or so it seemed.

"Listen, Simon, *you're* a writer." His voice had settled back
down to normal pitch, with the trace of a New Jersey accent.
"You know how damn hard it is to get published. And how
little you get paid when you do." I thought of that publisher
telling me to take fifty bucks or get fucked.

"But..."

"And I'm sure you're postmodern enough to understand
that 'the author' is just a construct, right?"

Okay, I knew of writers who invented personae in order to
get published—that young, urban gay male porn writer, for
instance, who was really a very straight middle-aged woman
living on a farm in Kansas. But this was different. This was *serious*. "Yeah," I mumbled, "but...exploiting abuse...AIDS...
homelessness...hustlers..."

4

JT LeRoy—or whoever—grabbed my shoulder, hard. "Get a fucking hold of yourself. *Lou Reed* reads my work in public. *You* can barely afford his CDs. What does that tell you about truth and authenticity, huh?"

"But JT, who is that little boy in the blond wig who appears...?"

"Simon, you can either forget your fucking principles and accept my honest praise—because I think you're a helluva writer, really—or you can *suck my dick.*" His hand pressed down on my shoulder. "Or both."

Now, anybody who's read my autobiographical work—which is really true nonfiction, by the way, not some self-serving invention like JT's, I swear—knows that I'm a top, but a top with a wide submissive streak. I willingly let myself be pushed to my knees.

JT LeRoy unbuttoned his 501s and reached inside. My mouth watered—I mean, it actually did, though whether for dick or for *famous* dick is open to debate.

The cock that appeared, still half-hooded in foreskin, was just a bit bigger than average, large enough to be a nice mouthful, small enough to deep-throat without gagging. Perfect. At that sacred moment, I didn't care whether JT LeRoy thought I could write or not. After all, lots of people can write passable gay porn: grannies with good imaginations, straight guys who wouldn't be caught dead actually touching a hard-on, me. But not everybody can suck cock. At least, not well. If there's one thing my decades of slutdom have taught me, it's that.

I happily licked swollen dickhead. JT LeRoy hadn't bathed for a while. I was well and truly turned on.

"That's it, you fucking freelance writer," the leatherman growled. "You suck that...notorious cock." Well, his boudoir chat was nowhere near as accomplished as his written prose, but no matter. I grabbed on to his cowhide-clad thighs and swallowed the swollen shaft, my tongue doing little tangos on the underside as I gulped it down.

"Mmm," said the man who was—maybe—JT LeRoy.

"Mmf," I replied.

I imagined myself as the JT LeRoy the world thought it knew: a fucked-up trailer-trash kid pimped out by his mommy, turning redneck tricks, being used and abused. Fuck. I sucked even harder. I wallowed in the now-familiar JT LeRoy mulch of hard-edged sexuality, Southern gothic, and innocence-lost sentimentality. It felt nice, even though my face was being fucked so hard that tears came to my eyes.

A big, strong hand came down on the back of my head, forcing me further onto his big, stiff dick. "That's it, you over-educated little fuck. Show me you understand what life is really about."

Well, that seemed like more of a philosophical challenge than I was up to at the moment, but I did my level best.

Okay, I almost never swallow. It's not that I think it's particularly risky. It's just that I cut back on my sperm intake a long time ago, and I never went back to indiscriminate cum-guzzling. But this was *JT LeRoy*, dammit, and when, with much grunting, he came, I chugged down every salty drop. It was, well, positively Whitmanesque. And if it wasn't Whitmanesque, not really, at least I'd gotten closer to the *real* JT than that shoplifter Wynona Ryder most likely ever would.

That was it. That was that. A blow-and-go. Not to be repeated, or even spoken of, though I would have been up for a rematch. But whenever JT wrote me afterward, he never referred to my giving him head. Same went for his phone calls—not a glimmer of the sex we'd had, just him asking for favors and sympathy in the same femmy Southern voice he'd always used. I didn't want to press the point. But it made me wonder whether the man who showed up at my door was the real fake JT, or a poseur posing as a poseur. Now *that* was postmodern.

I never told anyone about my blow-job brush with notoriety, figuring that my non-writer friends would, hurtfully, not care, while my fellow authors would reckon I made the whole thing up, spun out of whole, envious cloth, like I was aiming to hitch my wagon to a slutty star. So I was left to wonder, by myself, about the motives and veracity of would-be JT and his maybe-famous phallus.

And then, a couple of months after the suck job, the big JT LeRoy hoax story broke. An article in *New York* magazine led the way, followed by other exposés and equivocal confessions. It turned out that, no, JT LeRoy wasn't some young whore-turned-genius. He was, in fact, an almost-forty-year-old woman named Laura Albert. And oh, the shock, the gnashing of teeth, the reproach, the soul searching that gripped the world of queerish writers and otherwise edgy authors. As a few churlish observers pointed out, the story was strikingly similar to one that Armistead Maupin had written years before, *The Night Listener*, and so We Should Have Known Better. But, as with WMDs and transubstantiation, it's human nature to be willingly misled; countless generations of con artists have made big bucks by exploiting just that very thing.

I myself had mixed emotions. While I deplored the exploitation of HIV, abuse, and homelessness involved in "JT LeRoy's" rise to fame, the envy I'd had for JT's career now morphed into a kind of sullen admiration. It had taken balls to parlay a knack for writing into global notoriety, even if those balls belonged to a woman named Laura. Sure, I was sympathetic that a couple of my more-famous-than-me writer pals were distraught over being used, but hey, when they'd been involved in organizing proxy-JT events, they'd never invited *me* to read.

And anyway, I had career troubles of my own: more cuts in what had already been pathetically small fees, my online column being canned. My finances were increasingly shaky, my ego was in the toilet. I was thinking about giving up writing altogether, and taking up something more lucrative, like babysitting. Surprising, then—actually, much *more* than surprising—when I got another phone call from JT LeRoy.

"Simon?" the familiar femmy voice said. "This is JT."

"Um, uh…" I said.

The voice on the other end did a glissando down the scale, all the way down to a leatherman's toppish basso. "You were such an amazing cocksucker," he said. "The best." Was *that* true? Well, I wanted it to be. "So I've decided to fuck you. When's a good time?"

"Listen, JT…or whoever you really are…I just don't think…"

"I'll explain everything when I get over there. And I promise I'll fuck your ass but good."

Both my curiosity and my horniness were piqued, jostling for dominance in my forebrain. Sure, I was usually the one doing the topping, but if I *was* going to get fucked, I could imagine no one better suited to the job than Mr. Leather Whoever and his impressive erection.

And hey, it wasn't like Laura Albert had actually confessed to anything. The gun might have been warm and smelling of gunpowder, but it wasn't actually smoking, so maybe I was indeed going to get fucked by the really real JT. In any case, it was becoming increasingly indisputable that I was going to get fucked by *somebody*.

And, at base—let's face it—I wanted JT LeRoy to want me.

"Laura? Laura was just *my* front, though she did help out a little, with the Southern stuff mostly. Wheels within wheels, eh?" We were lying in bed together, my asshole pulsing with that just-fucked feeling. The leatherman continued, "I mean, how do you think JT knew all about the S/M hustling scene? And if you met JT and he turned out to be a middle-aged woman, what kind of a story would that be for you to tell?" (Or maybe he said "sell." I wasn't quite sure which.) "Not as hot as this one, Simon, not fucking nearly."

Well, the sex *had* been indisputably scorching. I'd been cleaned out and naked when the leatherman arrived. Within a couple of minutes—questions about veracity rendered irrelevant—I was on my back, looking up at my fucker's handsome, bearded face as he eased himself down into me. I don't get screwed very often, but I know how to relax, and I took the full length of his cock without a whimper. Men who have never been screwed may wonder, "How can getting fucked not hurt?" but the rest of us know it feels *great*.

"JT" was surprisingly gentle at first, until he'd guided himself inside me, but then the stroking turned to pistoning, and soon he was ramming away. I reached for his butt, in hopes my grasp would moderate his thrusts and keep him from tearing my hole apart. But fuck, it did feel amazing. My hands moved up, stroking his back; around to his hairy chest, pausing to play with his prominent nipples; then grabbing him around the neck, hungry for his kiss.

He obliged, and our tongues met. By that point, I'd totally surrendered to his cock pumping away in my ass, and I couldn't even wrap my mind around caring who the man inside me was. But then, do we ever know who our sex partners really are? Really?

And just when I thought I'd have to ask "JT" to back off and give me a rest, he said, sweat dripping from his face, "You want to come? I'm fucking close." So I nodded, reached down for my limpish cock, and tortured it till it hardened and got ready to shoot.

"Now," he said. "Now?"

"Yeah, JT. Go for it."

And we came at pretty much the same pornographic moment, him inside a regrettable-but-necessary condom, me all over my belly. He climbed off me and we wriggled round until we were lying side by side, panting, his strong arms wrapped around me. And, as soon as the spasms had subsided and we caught our breaths, he leaned over and whispered in my ear, "*That's* what life is about—fuck or get fucked."

I stared at him, not sure if I should try to kiss him again or not.

"And I have a film deal," he continued. "I'm going to be writing a screenplay, Laura's story. Well, actually she's the one who's going to be credited with it, but..."

"Profiting from a hoax, huh?"

"Well, *somebody* should." The scent of spent jism rose from our bodies.

I looked over at him, hopefully, ashamedly, and asked, more eagerly than was seemly, "So you need any help with the script?"

COMING TO GRIEF

Dale Chase

Jake ruined me for anybody else and when he didn't stick around, when he went and died on me, I wanted to die too, almost did one night and it would have been so easy to miss the turn and hit the wall but I didn't and now here I am with my dick in some poor sap who I didn't warn off but shoulda.

I can fuck but I hate it not bein Jake so I get rough which most like but sometimes a rough fuck ain't enough and I've been known to beat the shit out of people so mostly I jerk off. Thinkin of Jake. I can forget the bad part then, shut my eyes and shoot a load rememberin him suckin it down.

This guy I'm doin now says he's comin but I don't give a shit. He's just ass to me, place to put my dick and get off. I hold him at the hips, ram a few more times and feel the rise and *holy hell, mother fuck, Jesus god.*

When I'm done I pull out, toss the rubber, and look where I been, hate his hairy ass. I slap his butt and he falls over onto his side, grins at me which I want to wipe off his face but I hold back which is like holdin off a fuckin hurricane and I'm up and dressed and out the door before he can try to stop me which would get him the shit beat out of him.

In my truck I take a slug off a pint, then one more before I drive off. Should go home but don't because I can't stand it so I head out of town, get on the highway feelin like there was no fuck and I'm still lookin to come. And it makes me think back to Jake because when I did him it would pretty much level me and I'd wake up hours later with him beside me and not remember fallin asleep, only the fuck. That's gone now and I can fuck my goddamn brains out and it don't matter and I start to wonder if it's me holdin on to Jake or him holdin on to me.

I turn around and drive back and it's dawn by the time I pull in at the ranch where I beat hell out of Paul Dooley when I hear him sayin we're better off with Jake dead, "One less faggot." Then Claude Morton, the owner, takes me into his office, tells me I'm let go because I'm fightin too much, no good to him like that. "I understand what you been through," he says, "and I sympathize because Jake was a good man and I know you were close but you need to move on, Harley. You're killin yourself stayin here."

I want to hit him and he knows this but he don't back down, then he tells me he knows a man in California with a small cattle ranch on the coast and he's already called him and I can have a job there. "Cows graze right up to the ocean," Claude says but I don't give a shit about that because he's throwin me out and I can't leave Jake and he sees this. "You have to live your life now," he says. "Jake wouldn't want you to fold up over him."

I've heard about California and don't like any of it but I have no choice unless I want to scrape up work here, which ain't easy nowadays. Claude comes out from behind his desk, tries to put an arm around my shoulder but I shake him off.

"Okay, okay," he says like you do to a skittish horse. "Just think about it."

I ride out with the cattle later on and while I'm out there I stop and get out my dick and jerk off thinkin of Jake because we'd stop and fuck standin between the horses and they'd smell the sex and their dicks would get hard. Now I shoot under the horse's legs but by the time my come hits the ground I feel awful again and there is no fuckin end to it. Later, ridin back, I see what Claude means and when I tell him next day I'll take the California job he says it's best and I think how in hell do you know cause you never lost your man and I know you and Robert ain't brothers like you led everyone to believe all these years. It was Jake himself told me you were queer after he saw you fuckin, two old men still gettin it up—so I hate you tellin me what to do because you don't know, you don't know cause Robert's there in the house and you can go fuck soon as you're done cuttin me loose.

But I am cut and I pack what I have which ain't much and I stop by Jake's grave where I have not been able to go before, but now I do and say I'm sorry though I wasn't the drunk who plowed into him and died killin him but it feels that bad. There's weeds come up over Jake and I kneel down and pull em out, then tell him good-bye, and then drive to California where I get lost and end up at a truck-stop motel where I see boys gettin into the cabs for fucks but I jerk off instead, couple times.

Next day I find a town called Paso Robles which ain't bad, then drive from there to the coast where I see the ocean which is a sight and as I drive north to Cambria where the ranch is it comes and goes to my left and I smell it more than see it because it's down below the cliff. And then I see cows grazin at the edge and think Claude was right and I hate him for that.

I am given a job and allowed to bunk in a small trailer on the ranch, as the owner, Jim Merchant, seems to know my hard-luck story. The trailer is small and I think maybe I'd be better off outside on the ground but I work at settlin in as much as I can which ain't much.

Herdin stock in a Jeep is new to me but I do what I'm told and after that get some beers and go down to the ocean and sit on my truck fender and watch the sun set into the waves. It's like another country here and I feel out of place everywhere I go but can't tell if it's the place or me. Don't belong anymore, not without Jake.

Jim's a good man and I come to like workin for him but he tries to talk to me when I wish he wouldn't and I put him off more than not. Other hands mostly give me room; nights I jerk off in the trailer. Then I hear about San Francisco which you can drive north to and there's bars for everything you want so I go up there one Saturday and find myself in a back room gettin my dick sucked but when I try to fuck the guy he tells me he don't do that and there is almost a fight but others break it up and I leave. I go to another bar and men come around, call me cowboy, and I tell them I just want to fuck and I go home with one and fuck but he wants me to stay over and I can't do that so I leave, drive back to Cambria and my trailer. Sunday morning I jerk off, tell Jake maybe he's better off where he is, then go for a drive south, past Morro Bay and the big rock they've got, down to San Luis Obispo, one town runnin into another and none of it matters. I'm back for the sunset, sittin on my truck with my beer. A man runs past me wearin almost nothin, shorts and shoes. He nods as I look and I turn back to the sunset.

Next night he runs past again, nods, but I don't bite. Night after that he says, "Hey, cowboy," as he passes and I think if he'd stop I'd wipe that grin off his face. Then after a couple weeks of this he does stop when I wish he wouldn't but he keeps his distance and asks am I new to the area and I nod, think maybe he wants to fuck.

He gets it outta me I work on the ranch, tells me he's Gage Toland and teaches school which makes me laugh because I ain't fuckin no teacher and I tell him I'm Harley Knox and he seems to like that but he don't press, then runs on.

I drive up to San Francisco Saturday and get me a guy who's rough as me and we wrestle and fuck and wrestle some more but then he tries to stick his dick in me and I land a punch and all hell breaks loose and I drive back to Cambria bruised across the jaw. Jim Merchant don't comment when he sees the purple on Monday.

Goddamn runner, Gage, comes by the ocean every night so I finally offer him a beer which he drinks and I ask if that don't go against his runnin and he says yeah, probably, but he's earned it. I want to ask him what he wants of me, does he want to fuck, but ain't sure to do that out here. Then he says would I have a drink with him later on and tells me to meet him at some bar and I think okay, I'll drink with him and fuck him, so I agree. At the bar he's in a goddamn western shirt and boots which makes me laugh.

"You don't say much," he offers as we drink. I shrug. "It's appealing, you know," he says and there are a couple other things after that before I turn to him, tell him I am lookin to fuck and no more.

"Sure," he says. "You can come to my place." He starts out but I won't ride with him, take my truck and follow. Little house up on a hill behind another house. I park beside him, dick hard.

He's got the door open and I go inside and soon as he closes it, I start in at him, get his jeans down, get him on the floor, put on the rubber, spit myself wet, and do him. Don't look around, don't look nowhere but his ass where my dick is buried and where I want to tear his fuckin hole apart. He don't say nothin, just lets me ride it out, and when I come it's a gusher and I pump his butt full while I slap him and when I'm done I pull out and stand up, pull off the rubber, drop it, pull up my jeans. He rolls onto his back and he's workin his dick and lookin at me but I turn to leave, then hear him grunt so I look back over my shoulder and see the spunk and for a second I remember how Jake looked doin that after I'd fucked him and I want to stop this teacher, tell him he's makin the biggest fuckin mistake of his life, but I leave instead and in my truck find the pint in the glove box and have me a couple pulls. And next night I don't go to the ocean; I go to a bar and get drunk.

I hate the teacher takin away the ocean like that but the bar has windows at the back so I can see the sunset and I watch and drink, glad the day's done. Next night Gage finds me there, says he saw my truck out front and can he buy me a drink. It's all I can do to not get my dick out and fuck him then and there, turn him up onto the table and give it to him so hard he can't walk after. I feel it rise in me, hard dick yeah but along with it that somethin else that's hooked up now, ever since Jake, like fuckin has a price I keep payin but still keep owin.

I nod to the drink, consider just gettin drunk, but I know he wants to fuck because it comes across the table as sure as if it was a dick reachin out to me. Only good part is he don't talk. He looks from me to the sunset and I wonder how he sees it all but I don't know how to ask so I don't.

"Your hands are bruised," he says when the sun is down. "Hard work."

"Yeah."

It's there between us now, the fuck, and I don't want to talk about no work or nothin and I'm tired of holdin off and I am about ready to tell him this when he says we can go to his place. I tell him no, to come with me so he gets into my truck and I drive to the ranch and out a road to nowhere and stop there. "Get out," I say.

He does and I put him onto all fours in the truck bed and fuck him there with the cold air on my ass and it's a good god-damn fuck, I'll give him that. Don't know why, maybe for bein outside, and I don't think of nothin else while I do it which is maybe my way of bein at peace—with my dick up some ass—and I go at him hard but not rough like the others, don't want to beat hell out of him and don't know why, don't want to know, and when I come it's a relief, only when I pull out I think how he's the first I've done twice since Jake and I hate him for it but that don't feel good either.

He rolls over, sits up, says I drove the come out of him and how we're a good fit so there we are in the truck bed, sittin back on our haunches bare-dicked and I am fuckin lost and I look up to the stars and I goddamn want to howl. And Gage, who's smarter, teacher and all, says it's okay, it's okay, even though he don't know what's in me. Or maybe he does. Jake knew, just like I knew what was in him and we were different but where it matters we were the same.

"You're a puzzle, Harley Knox," Gage says as we pull up our pants and climb out of the truck bed. "You're like a force mowing down everything in its path and I find I can't keep from stepping in your way."

"Better if you did," I tell him and I feel somethin in me break with those words cause I know that force he talks about and it's near to knockin me down so instead of gettin in the truck and drivin away, I sit on the tailgate with everything fallin into a heap and when I look up at the trees I think they should be comin down too, it's that bad.

Gage sits down beside me but don't touch me, which is best as I don't think I could stand it but he does ask a question. He asks me what happened. No when or where, just what it is, and I see how he's slippin in through the break in me and I think to stop him only I don't. And then I tell him.

"I come from Texas and when I was eighteen I got a job on a cattle ranch and another guy did too, one year older, Jake Colley, and we became friends. And more." Here I have to stop because it's Jake and me only I'm with somebody else and I have to give that a minute. Then I go on. "Four years workin together and everything else, you know, then one night a drunk driver crosses the line doin seventy and hits Jake head-on, kills them both and me too only I wasn't there so I'm still walkin around dead. I went kinda crazy after that so I was let go from the job but the owner got me the job here, said I'd best get on with life which I have only I'm caught in between, not there but not here neither."

"I am so sorry," Gage says.

"Not your fault."

"I know, I'm just sorry you've had such a loss."

I don't know what to say next because now he's gotten inside me where he don't belong and I see I shoulda stayed quiet about all of it. I don't want his sorry so I get up, say we need to go. I take him back to his car and before he gets out of my truck he says he'd like to see me again.

"Can't do that," I tell him, which is the truth.

He thinks a second, then tries again. "No strings, just sex if that's what you want."

I'm not sure about this but I do want to fuck him again. "You know where to find me," I say and he gets out and I drive to my trailer. Next day I'm back out with the cattle at the edge of the ocean and I bring Jake to mind because he'd of liked this, sittin in the Jeep wonderin if a cow ever slips and falls into the ocean. We'd laugh about the cow on the way down thinkin *Oh shit*. And we'd fuck, maybe there in the Jeep. And I think of how it feels gettin into him from behind, ridin out a good come, and this gets my dick hard so I get it out cause nobody's around but the cows and I jerk off looking at the ocean but seein Jake. Then later when I'm drivin across the highway a string of people on bicycles all wearin helmets and shorts goes by and Gage comes to mind when I wish he wouldn't. But that night I go to the ocean and he runs up and without a word we get into the truck bed and fuck under a blanket so nobody can see.

This happens a bunch more times over the next few weeks and he don't say a word, just lets me fuck him and there's come all over the truck bed from him shootin while I do him and the dogs at the ranch start jumpin up there sniffin around and so I have to hose it out and one night after we fuck I tell Gage this which makes him laugh.

"That's the first thing you've said in weeks," he says which I know but it still embarrasses me and I tell him I'm not good with words, never finished school.

"That doesn't matter," he says. "A lot of men are reserved with what they say. I've found when they do choose to speak, it's usually worthwhile compared to ones who prattle away about nothing."

I don't know what to say to this. We're still under the blanket, it's dark now and Gage runs a hand onto my chest. "You have a wonderful body," he says, "and the best part is it's not cultivated at some gym."

"Cultivated." I chuckle at this and he does too.

"You're the real thing, Harley, more than most. I don't think you realize your appeal."

Just then a car pulls alongside and we freeze. They turn off the lights and nobody moves so they're like us, come down to watch the ocean, probably not to fuck though. "What now?" Gage says and I tell him to follow me and we pull our pants up while under the blanket, then stay low and slide out of the truck, fall to the ground, go around the far side then make like we've just walked back from somewhere. We get in and drive away and Gage laughs like hell.

I take him home and when he asks me in I say no and we go on like this a while longer, fuck in the truck every night after sunset which I like but then he says a bed ain't so bad and if I'd stick around there's more than a quick fuck. "Sex can go on for hours," he tells me and I like the sound of that, but also don't. Much as I want it, it also grates on me in a way I can't tell him because I'm not sure I know but he keeps on about it, then one Friday night when I've got a pint instead of beer and have downed about half, I go home with him where he asks me to suck his dick.

I look at him standing there with it hard and see what I haven't really looked at before, how his chest is smooth, no hair, and he's lean but muscled and down below his hair is darker than mine and his dick is dribbling juice and I fix on this because I remember Jake that way and he had black hair down there too and that sweet dick. I'd suck him sometimes and he'd come in my mouth and callin this up ain't my fault, it's Jake still in me and I can't suck no cock and I grab Gage, push him onto the bed, fuck him hard. He don't fight and he comes into the sheets and when we're done he turns over and looks me in the eye and I see it's not gonna work like he said and I get up, find my jeans.

He makes a mistake then, puts a hand on me as if to stop me, and I turn, shove him back onto the bed.

"Harley," he says.

"Don't say it," I tell him. "Don't."

But he does and I dress and he keeps on until I want to hit him. "Don't," I say again and he stops. Then when I'm at the door, him still naked, he says, "Harley, when are you going to allow yourself to live? You're not the one who died," and I slug him in the gut but instead of foldin up like I expect, he lands a punch just below my eye which knocks me back but not off my feet and I light into him and we go at it until I've got him on the floor, on his back, and he says to me "You can't beat it out of me. How I feel is how I feel and I want you, Harley, god how I want you. Why's that so wrong?"

I have no ready answer besides Jake and he's dead so I know that's not the answer I can give and I am stopped in my tracks.

I look down at Gage who slowly opens his arms which causes me to back off and get up. He just lies there on the floor, bruise already coming up on his cheek, blood at the corner of his mouth, and he takes hold of his dick, starts to work it, and there it is. I hate how it is but I can't not do it and I get down there and suck him and he pulls at me so I slide around, let him get mine out and we lie there on the floor suckin dick but we don't come. Then he pulls off after a while, plays with me, handles my balls, and says how good it is but there's more to life than sex which is a laugh as I've got his dick in my mouth. So I pull off and sit up and he says to undress and I do. I crawl onto him, dicks between us, and we roll around some and it gets wet between us and the smell is like in the truck and I think of the dogs sniffin us.

"I want to explore you, Harley," Gage says as he runs a hand down onto my ass, squeezes me. "I want to know every part of you but right now, before that, I want you to fuck me."

I sit back and he raises up his legs and I see he wants it from the front which is new to me but I get on a rubber and he's holdin himself open so his hole is there to see and I put my dick into it, then look up at him. So I fuck while he watches me and I can see on his face how it feels for him. And he says, "It's okay," and I think *No it's not* but then I'm gonna come.

BENEDICTION

Alana Noel Voth

I'm naked. I can't see anything; it's dark. I hope I'm in Cheeseman Park. Mom and I used to go there with Mom's friend, Ryan. We'd sit at a picnic table and eat chicken and salad. I remember one time after lunch, I was like seven, I went down the slide on my belly just to get that rush in my gut—that thrill of being, for one second, out of control, rushing headlong at the gravel with my hands out and face forward. Later, I buried my legs in the sand, and then my knees rose from the dead.

I used to look at pictures of men in *GQ* and *Esquire* and wonder what it would take to get a man to love me. I was ten and obsessed with love. Ryan found me gazing at a black-and-white spread of a male model once and said, "Brenner, what are you looking at?"

I pointed at the male model.

"Listen, Brenner. You like guys; that's okay. I want you to know it's okay. Your mom loves you. I love you too. I'm gay. You knew that. Right. So listen, I don't want to scare you, but it can be...complicated. Know what I mean?"

Mom loved me.

Ryan loved me.

I believed someone else would love me too.

Not that I lived in a perfect world. Grand Junction wasn't a gay boy's Utopia. I knew the most insulting thing you could do was call a guy a faggot. By the time I was in kindergarten I knew you could be a leper or a homo, there wasn't much difference. In first grade, I sealed my fate. I told my classmates when I grew up I'd write books and marry a man. I was by myself after that. Always. Teachers expected me to be attentive and get good grades but then looked at me like I had a booger on my finger and was going to wipe it on them.

It's dark. I'm naked and lying on some grass; I must be in Cheeseman Park, because I feel the grass blades like a cool prickly blanket beneath my skin. I used to lie in the backyard with nothing on and enjoy the tickle of grass against my ass and shoulders. A sprinkler would come by and douse me with mist. I lay there and played with my dick. My dick would get hard and even have a feeling like coming, except nothing would come out, no jizz.

I'll imagine my lungs are an accordion—you know, those things that a person plays by pushing it in and then pulling it out and it makes noise like wheezy music.

In and out, in and out, that's good, that's good; keep it going.

I hear an owl hooting and try and hoot back. I've always wanted to do that. I can't. Maybe I gurgled. Is it late? I want to feel the sun on my face. I don't want to be scared. Oh fuck, I'm scared. I miss Ron. Everything hurts: My chest, my throat, my whole body. Feels like I got thrown around in a car. I remember a car going fast. A car accident? They say your life flashes before your eyes. Maybe I should close mine.

I used to close my eyes in Mom's car. She liked driving her convertible Volkswagen Beetle with the top down. Sometimes we'd drive through town—Mom with her blonde hair blowing behind her, and me waving at everyone like they were friends.

On the stereo, Johnny Cash sang: *Love is a burning thing, and it makes a fiery ring, bound by wild desire; I fell into a ring of fire.*

When I was in sixth grade, Ron McDermott and some other guys were in someone's garage playing with matches and gasoline. Something about *they were going to build the biggest most terrifying bonfire any man had ever seen!* Then Ron went up in flames and according to some reports was ruined, destroyed, painful to look at, to see. He spent months in the hospital having skin grafts and physical therapy and still he was badly scarred.

When Ron came back to school, he wore a flesh-colored bodysuit under his clothes and one half of his face was red and swollen. He did look a little lopsided. Mostly he looked sad. Other kids avoided him or stared when they thought he wasn't looking, which made me mad, made me defensive.

But something else.

Part of me, an inside thing, like a spirit or an emotion, *something eternal* reached out to him, wanted to touch Ron, comfort him, and make him smile again. I recognized another tortured soul, I guess, another straggler, black sheep, leper.

I approached him one day on the playground.

"Want to play tetherball or something?"

Ron McDermott looked at me. He wore a hat, I think to keep his scars out of the sun, which made me sorry because I loved the feel of the sun on my face.

"I'm not supposed to," he said. "Moving too much stretches my scars then they hurt or they might tear, then I'd have to get more grafts and that sucks."

"Oh." I hadn't thought of that. I felt stupid. "I'm really not into tetherball. I mean what's the point?" I laughed, shaking my head, trying to make him feel comfortable, trying to relax. "What about jacks?"

"Jacks?"

"Yeah, with the ball and the jacks...."

Ron raised one eyebrow. He had perfect eyebrows. They hadn't been burned off. He also had beautiful eyes—very green.

"Isn't that like a girl's game?" he said.

I shrugged. "Is it?"

Come to think of it, I'd only played jacks with girls, mostly Jill and Susanne, who didn't drive me crazy saying, "I wish you weren't gay, Brenner," and "What a waste," or "C'mon, Brent, kiss me. See what you think."

Why did I have to do that? So I'd be normal, okay?

Ron smiled. "It's totally a chick game."

I laughed. "Guess so."

After a moment Ron cracked a smile.

We were together after that—a gruesome twosome. Insepa-rable, coconspirators, buddies. When teachers said our names out loud it was always "Brent and Ron" or "Ron and Brent," but never just one or the other.

One day Ron said, "I'm happy we're friends." Then he punched me in the shoulder.

I rubbed my shoulder then punched him back. "Me too."

To tell the truth, he was my soul mate, my other half.

And you can weather any storm like that. Face any demon.

We hung out and listened to music. Ryan was constantly giv-ing me old stuff, so Ron and I made mix tapes, odd compila-tions like "Why Me?" by Planet P followed by "Dreaming" by Blondie, then "Lola" by the Kinks, and then "New Moon on Monday" by Duran Duran, and then "Ballroom Blitz" by Sweet. I'd dance to that one, get goofy bouncing around and shaking and doing the robot, and Ron would sit on the floor near the cassette player and laugh.

I loved his laugh; it was a musical kind of sexy laugh. It egged me on. I'd get goofier just to hear him.

Sometimes Ron would drum a beat on his legs or shake his head so his bangs flopped. He couldn't dance because he still had to watch what he did physically, and his movements were limited, like he couldn't lift his arms too high because the bands of new skin they'd put on him were still tight. He said it felt like wearing a shirt that was too small. He said he felt like a retard because of his physical limitations, because he had to go to therapy with kids who were missing limbs and wore leg braces, and because every morning he had to strip down in front of his mother so she could rub lotion into his scars.

"I feel like an ugly retard," he told me one afternoon. We were in my room on the floor surrounded by tapes.

"You're not ugly." I told him. Not to me he wasn't. I pawed through the cassettes and found something new, the Goo Goo Dolls, and put it into the player.

"C'mon," Ron said. "You see how people look at me—like I'm Frankenstein. No girl is ever going to touch me. All I'm ever going to get is my mom rubbing lotion on me." He put his face in his hands. "No girl is ever going to touch me." He started to sob—a hoarse wretched sound that twisted my gut and broke my heart. "I'll be like that guy in *Mask*," he choked. "He's so ugly his mother has to buy him a hooker."

What did I say? *It's not true. You're not ugly. Forget girls.*

"I'll do it," I said.

"Do what?" Ron lifted his face. Tears and snot glistened across his red scars.

"I'd touch you. I mean, you know, rub lotion on you."

He wiped his nose on his sleeve. "What?"

"I'd do it if you want."

Ron stared at me. "You're just trying to make me feel better."

"No," I said.

We went quiet, listening to the tape.

We had a sleepover once. I stayed the night at his house. We stayed up until three watching MTV then *The Sixth Sense* on video and then getting freaked out by the movie and talking about whether it would be possible to talk to the dead. We also made plans to go to the same college. Ron wanted to become a plastic surgeon and help other kids who were burned. I wanted to be a writer and write love poems.

The next morning, Ron's mother called him downstairs so she could rub lotion on him. He looked at me. I nodded like, okay, go. After a while, I couldn't help it. I wandered from his room down the hallway, down the stairs and then around the house until I found the door to the room open. Spare bedroom, I guessed. Ron lay on a bed. Nothing but a sheet on a mattress.

He was naked on his stomach with his head turned toward the wall, maybe staring at the swirls of paint and seeing pictures—maybe himself not burned. I sucked in my breath. He was nearly skeletal, so thin, and his skin was a twist of stark white and purple, like a candy cane. His mother sat on the edge of the bed and leaned over him, working lotion into his scars: Across his shoulders, down each arm, and then to the slope of his back. His ass was white and round. I felt the forceful stir of my erection. His mother concentrated on what she was doing, tending her wounded boy. I knew then I wanted to tend him too: I'd do anything. Ron turned his head and saw me. My heart waved. After a moment he barely lifted a hand and wriggled his fingers at me. I nodded then backed out of the door.

It was the summer after eighth grade when Ron told me, "I was so fucking glad when I was conscious enough in that dumb hospital to look down and see my dick was there. It wasn't burned off."

He sighed and looked truly relieved.

"Yeah, I know what you mean."

I began to wonder about Ron's dick. Short and fat; long and curved? Average length? Ethereal? Did hair grow around his balls? What did his balls smell like? Would his come taste like rice pudding?

"There was a nurse that really turned me on there."

"What?" I'd been lost in a daydream.

"A nurse," Ron repeated. "A couple times I beat off in my hospital bed, under the sheets, thinking about her tits."

We were in Ron's room. The window was open. A cool breeze drifted in and tickled my skin. From the cassette player Melissa Etheridge sang, *I'm the only one to walk across a fire for you.*

"Really?" I'd beat off plenty of times thinking about Ron.

"Guess you don't think about chicks," Ron said.

"Umm, no…" I laughed. Dorky nervous laughter.

"What do you think about then?"

Another laugh. "I don't know."

"Is it a particular guy or something?"

"Why?" My heart had begun to beat faster. Maybe he wanted me to say I thought about him when I beat off.

"Tell me," Ron said.

"Okay." But then I didn't say anything.

"C'mon. What's the matter?"

I finally came up with something. "Circle jerks."

"What's a circle jerk?" Ron laughed.

"Guys jerking off in front of each other." I started to laugh again, really nervous. Really hopeful.

"No shit." Ron seemed to think about it. "You ever do it?"

"No."

"Why not?"

"I don't know."

"Never met any guys who wanted to?"

"I guess." I could feel my armpits sweating, my arms shaking, and my dick had started to move. I ran my hand through my hair, trying to think about something else—the rain in

Spain, something.

"Want to?" Ron asked.

"What?" Had my voice changed an octave?

"Jerk off."

I looked at him. "You want to jerk off in front of me?"

He was quiet. Then he said, "Well yeah. I mean I'm not queer. We're just friends, and I trust you."

Maybe he just didn't think he was queer.

I stared at him until my eyes watered. After a while Ron unzipped but didn't pull his dick out. Mine was already hard. I couldn't see his. Was he hard?

I unzipped. I had a nice dick, average length and all. I wanted Ron to look at it, want it. He looked for a minute then pulled his dick out. It was hard and as sweet as I'd seen in my dreams, average length but thick; his pubes were dark, and his balls looked heavy. I wished I could inhale his balls, lick them. Oh god. I began to jerk off. We jerked in unison. I'd never done this with anyone. I felt exposed and wished we were closer together. If I moved a little...there, our knees touched. I leaned back, pulling on my dick, teasing the head with my thumb. I pressed my knee against his. Ron looked at me.

"Oh god," I said. "Shit." I was going to come.

"Go," he said. "Shoot."

It was almost invisible to the naked eye, the eighth color of the rainbow, actually. Our come in the air together.

"Curtis Winters," I told him one afternoon that same summer. "Peewee baseball. I never saw a guy move like that. Looking at him gave me a stomachache."

Ron nodded. "April Reynolds. Before I got burned. She had long hair and this awesome smile. I wanted to feel her up."

He looked defeated, thinking about April Whoever, thinking about girls. I figured it was my duty to make him feel better since I was secretly madly in love with him. "Lie back," I said.

Ron lay back. I lay next to him, heart beating.

"Close your eyes. I'll close mine."

"Yeah, okay."

"Think of April, what's her name?"

"Reynolds."

"Yeah, think of her."

"Okay."

"What's she doing?" *The bitch*.

"Sitting in the desk across me in Ms. Morgan's class."

"And you're checking her out?"

"Well, yeah. Always."

"Imagine she wants to kiss you." Maybe I didn't sound enthusiastic enough. "She wants to suck your face off." I could smell Ron's hair, his shampoo, the lotion his mother rubbed in his skin. "Imagine soft lips and a warm tongue," I whispered.

Ron turned his head toward me. We were close enough to share breath. When he blinked I could have sworn I felt the soft flap of his eyelashes. I heard when he unzipped his pants, and then he grabbed my head and pulled me toward him.

I hesitated. "You really want to?"

"Do you want to?"

"Yeah."

"I'm not queer," he said, "I just want you to do it."

God, oh god, at last. I opened my mouth then my throat and then eased my mouth down his shaft and felt the ridges and veins against my tongue and tasted his salty skin.

I sucked and licked and slobbered.

Ron lifted his hips off the bed, fucking me in the mouth.

I stopped and looked at him. "Ron?" I wiped the saliva off my chin.

He leaned back on his elbows, breathing heavy. Pre-come bubbled on the head of his dick. "What, what is it?"

"I don't know," I said at last. I took hold of his cock again and then pushed my face to his balls and breathed him.

He put his hand on my head. "It's okay," he said.

I hadn't realized I was crying a little.

By high school, you could barely tell Ron had been burned. He had a few scars on his face, more on his back and arms, but they weren't as red or angry looking anymore, not swollen. He stood taller in the hallways and met people's eyes. Once in the lunchroom he slapped some guy a high five. "Who was that?" I asked.

Ron shrugged. "Some guy in my geology class."

"The walls in the john have been newly decorated," I said. "Have you seen it?"

"Nah, I don't think so. What is it?"

"Brent Johnson is a flaming fucking faggot."

Ron shook his head.

"Careful, I might be contagious," I said, nudging him in the side.

He smiled. "Yeah, whatever. Just ignore that shit."

Girls looked at him. I saw them looking at him. They finally saw what I saw. Ron-beautiful-Ron with his thick dark hair and green eyes. His beauty gave me a stomachache sometimes. I'd call him on the phone just to hear his voice. I asked him all the time about college.

One afternoon I said, "What about CU in Boulder?"

Ron looked at me and then said, "Let's get the hell out of here," and I said, "All right," and we walked out of the school building to a lone willow tree that grew past the parking lot. I had him all to myself now and stared at the sky and said, "It's gorgeous."

The willow tree wept branches near a chain-link fence that encircled a field of cattails and wildflowers behind us. Ron shook two cigarettes from a pack of Marlboro Reds. "Here." He offered me one.

I sniffed the end, bittersweet.

Ron held out a lighter, a little unsteady, the flame flickering, and we met eyes over the fire. I wanted to say, "I love you, man." *I love you.* But I inhaled instead, and the butt of my cigarette gave way to ember, and I coughed.

Ron looked away, lighting his smoke. He turned his eyes to the willow then leaned back, his hair falling into his eyes. With one hand, I touched his elbow. He crossed his arms over his chest, didn't say anything, and didn't look at me either.

The sun has come up. But the air feels cold on my skin, biting, because I'm naked and hurt and here alone. It hurts to shiver. It hurts to think and remember. I can't move voluntarily. Just shiver. I stare through the tree at the sky and then stare at the leaves on the tree and try to focus and wish for the leaves to fall and coat me.

The natural process of breathing is agony. Was he like that, really, Ron groping a girl? When I turn my head, I see my clothes lying on the grass beside me. Ten hours ago, I was driving. I drove Mom's car off an interstate and onto this winding path of asphalt with road signs warning NARROW ROAD and NO PASSING. I had a map beside me, but the map had been handwritten and then photocopied, and things were scratched out and written over. I couldn't exactly read it. I wasn't sure I wanted to go to a party anyway. SENIOR BASH! GRADUATION! I surveyed the road ahead of me and thought how it was the sort of road where if I were trapped in a horror movie, I would happen upon a hitchhiker with an axe, or someone possessed by a demon speeding up to run me over.

A few miles later, I pulled over and sat at the wheel and took a deep breath. Was I ready to see him? What would I see? These past three months, we hadn't talked much. He had excuses not to get together. I got out of the car and started walking. I stuffed my hands in my pockets. Was he going to break my heart?

A white glow floated ahead and became a sign through the trees. *TRESPASSERS WILL GET A FOOT UP YOUR ASS.* The red letters were scrawled over white paint peeling away to reveal blond wood. I stopped, looking at it, and thought about turning back, getting in my car, going home. Mom and I could do something—get ice cream, watch a movie, play cards. Big deal, I was graduating high school.

Maybe I should call Ryan and ask for advice. *How to get over a man?* No, better: *How to make him love me.*

The no trespassing sign was hung on a barbed wire fence. I pulled the wire apart and then stuck one leg through, twisting my body beneath it then through it. I heard music and tracked the thump across the meadow to another border of trees. When I came out past the trees, I stared into the smoky heat from a bonfire and wondered if Ron was right there standing close to the flame?

Jill rushed up and hugged me then gave me a beer. She was with another girl. I didn't see Ron. Jill talked. "We thought we'd stay here awhile then head back to town and go to that bar, remember?"

I nodded.

"You drove, right?"

I nodded again.

"Where's your car?"

I jerked my head toward the orchard.

"You came the back way?"

"Yeah, I guess."

"Jill says they don't card at this bar," the other girl said.

I saw him. Ron with a chick. He had his arm around her. She had one hand in his back pocket, squeezing his ass.

Sometimes, I could still taste his come in my mouth.

Jill nudged me. I pretended to focus on finishing my beer.

"Brent," she said. "Brenner?"

"Think I could get another beer?" I asked.

"Don't go anywhere," she said before heading off.

I headed in Ron's direction. "Hey," I said when I reached him.

Ron smiled and then looked at the girl and said, "This is Brent."

She smiled, a little.

"Can I talk to you?" I asked him, ignoring her.

"Yeah, what about?" He had a blank face, no expression.

"Alone. Over there." I nodded over my shoulder.

The girl snaked her arm around his waist.

"I'm kind of with Connie," he said. "How about later?"

"Well, I kind of need to talk to you now."

The girl glared at me.

"Yeah, okay." Ron walked a few feet away. I followed.

"What are you doing?" I asked him.

Ron looked over my shoulder. "Kind of on a date." He smiled.

I moved close and pushed my face in his neck and held him. "I miss you," I said.

"Ron?" The girl was back.

He pushed me away, but I didn't go too far. "I love you," I said. "Okay? I want you to know that."

The girl stood next to Ron. "What? Are you some kind of faggot?"

Ron looked nervous. "We'll talk some other time, okay?"

I stepped forward again and grabbed him by the head and stared in his eyes and wouldn't let go. "It's me," I said. "Brent."

Ron held me back by the collar. "Stop it, okay? Just stop."

"Let's go," the girl said.

Other people stood around gawking. "Hey McDermott, Connie! You in or not?" Some guys a few yards away were waving to them, waiting. They looked at me, and the look said, *You're not invited.*

For one second, we locked eyes, Ron and me.

"Fuck you," I said.

He leaned over and whispered, "I didn't choose to be a freak, Brent. You did."

I stood there unable to move or speak. The girl wrapped her arms around his shoulders. He disappeared in a smudge of smoke and heat. People walked by, gawking and smiling. I didn't care. I hated them. Then I noticed a guy sitting on the back of a truck by himself. Blond as sunshine, alone. He looked me over then looked away. What the hell? I walked over and stared at him.

"What are you looking at?" he said.

"Nothing."

"Yeah, right."

I could have walked away. He grabbed my arm at the wrist. "Lover's spat?"

"What? Fuck no." I felt mean now, spiteful. There was something dangerous about this guy; I knew it and got a chill but then followed him anyway.

I love it when men kiss. Eye contact first. Then shared breath. Gentle lips. A little tongue. More lips. More tongue. They suck each other's lips. Whirl their tongues around. Moaning. They hold each other's heads. They get rough. Or they're gentle.

I was shoved into a car from behind. Two hands on the back of my head. My forehead hit the roof as I went. Then I was shoved into a seated position on the backseat. The car began moving. Two guys sat on either side of me. Up front, the guy I'd been kissing was driving. Another guy in the front looked over the seat at me.

"What the fuck you looking at?"

I looked away.

They started talking.

"Let's dump him in the faggot park."

"Yeah, the dumb fuck."

I started crying.

The guys in back began slugging me with their fists.

I had a pet rat once. Daxter. He got sick. His pale-yellow sides heaved as he struggled for breath, and red stuff leaked from his eyeballs. I touched his fur with my fingertip, and he squeaked. I touched him again, and he squeaked. I wanted to hold him, comfort him, except when I touched him, he squeaked. Then he began trying to drag himself away from me. So I wouldn't touch him.

I tried to drag myself away from them. They kept kicking and slugging me. I begged them to leave me alone.

Sunlight. I feel it on my face and imagine a perfect circle around me, like a circle they draw in voodoo to protect or keep evil spirits away. How long will I last? Where am I bleeding? Mom? I see her patching a hole in the knee of my jeans, which is weird, because I haven't worn those jeans since I was ten. I watch her work the needle into the denim, pull the thread out, work the needle into the denim, pull the thread out. *Mom, I can't wear those jeans anymore.* I hear voices. I try to say something. *Over here, the naked beaten boy.*

Someone is above me like a streak of white light before becoming a face. I don't know him. Should I fight? Is it over?

I feel a hand cupping my forehead, a warm touch. "We've got you now," he says. "You're all right. Can you hear me?"

There's this song by Madonna. One of the lines goes *We only hurt the ones we love.* I want to ask this person above me, *Do you think Ron loves me?* But I can't spit the words out, only a little blood.

SUCKSLUTS ANONYMOUS

Scott D. Pomfret

"Hi. My name is Michael. I'm a suckslut."

"Hi, Michael!" booms a chorus of male voices.

Michael is standing at a lectern positioned at twelve o'clock in a circle of folding chairs in the yellowed basement of a UCC church. On the wall hang children's drawings of the Hindu gods and goddesses. There's burnt coffee on the folding table and Styrofoam cups in towers. A dense pall of smoke lingers near the ceiling lamps. The other men look back impassively.

Michael is handsome, with a round head, early salt-and-pepper hair, and maybe too much chin. It makes him look cartoonish, like a superhero. It's his first time at the lectern after listening to other tales of cock-induced misery—the heartache, the chapped lips, the beloved pet Pekinese ruthlessly used to attract *what's your doggie's name*-type men in the park.

"Here's how bad I am. On my way over here, there was this hot doorman at the Plaza. Tall, dark skinned, Hispanic maybe. He was wearing one of those frock coats, an old-fashioned bandleader sort of uniform with the epaulettes and the gold braid. Standing, legs apart. A fucking colossus. Thighs like a speed skater. The two sides of his long coat were spread wide. His pants were tight as a bullfighter's. He jerked his head toward the valet booth, where they keep all the guests' car keys."

One of the men calls out, "Admit you're powerless against your addiction!"

"Submit to a higher power," says Gerry, Michael's sponsor. He's a stern, gray eminence with an oversized mouth.

"I explained to the doorman that I don't suck cock anymore, that I'm going to meetings and moving along on the road to recovery. He hauled out this slender rock-hard member. Eleven inches. No shit! I've seen a lot of cock in my day. I've sucked off the so-called baby's forearms and donkey dicks. Trust me. I don't exaggerate. It had a dark, almost purple tip. On the underside was a thick blue vein that had its own pulse. I flicked it with my tongue until the shaft was slicked and shiny. His crotch had a stale, mossy smell from the heat and sweat."

One of the men in the circle of folding chairs interrupts. "That's it," he says. "Bare your…" he takes a long drag on his cigarette before he adds weakly, "…soul."

Michael picks up where he was interrupted. "'Stop fucking around,' the doorman growled, 'and suck it.' So I did. I put my mouth over the tip and got down. It touched the back of my throat before I was halfway down the shaft. His cock throbbed and jumped. His thrust cracked my head back against the underside of the counter. 'Touch my balls,' he said. I cupped his sac, lifted his balls, rolled and kneaded. With my other hand, I grabbed the shaft. I did it as much for my balance as for his pleasure. He was pressing against my head, threatening to knock me over."

A few brothers slink in late, wiping the jizz from the corners of their mouths. Someone eases over and welcomes them to the meeting. Not a single one of them catches anyone's eye. Not even the one Michael had just exchanged blow jobs with in the utility closet braves a second glance.

"I dug fingers into his asscrack. He had a real StairMaster ass. I pulled it apart, slid my fingers into the heat and moisture. My ring finger touched his anus. He moaned and arched back. I pulled him into me, forcing his cock deep into my throat." Michael's hands perform a pantomime above the lectern that every eye in the room follows as closely as a child watching shadow puppets.

"Then he pulled away. He slid the engorged mushroom cap across my glistening lips as he jerked himself off. He was not looking at me so much as at his own member. Then suddenly he spasmed and thrusted. Wet spunk coated my lips and nose and cheekbones. Another spurt reached my forehead, stuck in my hair. Wet, sloppy chunks exploded all over the place; I caught them in my mouth like they were a first snowfall. At that moment, we both heard the voice that might have been speaking for some time already: 'May I have my Mercedes, please?' "

Michael glances at the circle of men. His face is full of rueful shame. "That's how bad I am. I truly am a suckslut. I admit it: I've lost control."

Faces in the front row nod in recognition. Sympathy. Someone walks over to Michael and gives him a hug.

"What'd you do then?"

"Well, *obviously*, I gave the guy in the Mercedes head in return for a ride over here. I *had* to. I was worried I was going
to be late."

Glances are exchanged. There's some perturbation in the
ranks.

"Thank you for that introduction, Michael," Gerry says.
"What else do you feel compelled to share with us tonight?"

"Um…well, first, I don't think of myself as a victim," Michael responds. "I'm a person who has the power to choose
my behavior."

"Absofuckinglutely," someone calls out, but a dozen men
who don't really believe in the piety fidget in their seats. Someone swears after burning himself on an errant splash of coffee.

"I do truly believe I was born a suckslut." Michael's breathing has gotten easier, and there's an arrogant edge to the way
he carries on. He surveys the room. "I sucked my thumb in the
delivery room when there was nothing else to turn to. Teachers and babysitters used to remark on my perseverance. I wore
my pacifier to a nubbin. As a child, I could suck the color off a
lollipop. Everlasting gobstoppers lasted me about ten seconds.
Popsicles didn't have a chance to melt in my mouth. Chrome
off a trailer hitch? You betcha. Every Boy Scout leader this side
of the Mississippi wanted me in his den."

Michael bangs the top of the podium with an open palm.
Many in the audience jump and look guilty. Others are staring
at the movements of Michael's mouth; from the looks on their
faces, it's easy to see there's just one thing on their minds.

"On my eighteenth birthday," Michael says, "I sucked off the entire starting line-up of the boys' varsity basketball team—at a single sitting. I spent a summer at the beach doing nothing but inflating rubber rafts; I put the electric air pump to shame."

Michael's face is earnest, his mouth grim. "I am not proud of these things," he says, yet he sounds proud. "But the best I ever had? It was a nineteen-year-old Mormon hoops player, size sixteen shoes. A kid who had never before had his dick sucked. I got him naked in the towel room at a resort where he was playing a tournament. A quick compliment, maybe two, and he was showing me everything the good lord had given him. Like all young men's, his cock was perfectly perpendicular, tight as a tuning fork. And he was so damn proud of it, like a little boy who'd just won the spelling bee. He was eager to show me how his new toy worked. I swear, the load he shot into me, he'd been saving since puberty."

Michael lowers his head and swallows deeply.

"I know it's wrong," he says. "Not everything is about sucking a stiffy. There's lots of other tremendously important things in life...ahem...like, uh, um. Well, I'm having trouble thinking of any. But there are, I'm sure. It's just that, well, a party without swinging dick—it makes me nervous."

"Amen!" shouts somebody in the circle.

"I'm *soothed* by dick," Michael says. He grips both sides of the lectern. He runs his palms rhythmically up and down the polished edge. He lets his fingertips gently caress and adjust the microphone stem. "Swinging dick in loose trousers—like a metronome counting down the minutes until someone blows a load down my throat. You know what I'm talking about."

There's a murmur of something like assent. Something knowing and brotherly.

"I look at cock in the locker room. I check it out in the shower. I look at it in the urinal. I am the nightmare of every straight man with the Irish curse." He grips both sides of the lectern as if he might vault himself over it. "My experience is that men like to show off their cocks."

There's an audible cheer this time, but everyone looks as if he's asking himself: *Is a cheer permitted? Shouldn't we be ashamed of this?*

"You know what I'm talking about!"

Now there's an unabashed and thoroughly lusty cheer. Michael steps away from the lectern. He paces the room like a maniac. "There are boys who like it up the ass. There are boys who like to watch. Boys who like toys. But me...my vice? I'm a suckslut. I love cock."

He looks at them defiantly. Is anyone going to dare to stir, to yawn, to express anything but loving approbation?

"It doesn't mean you're a bad person," someone calls out.

"No way!" says someone else. It's a very supportive environment.

Michael's hand burrows deep in his pocket. He squeezes his erection through the cloth.

"Michael," Gerry says. There's a tremor in his voice. "I think we're beginning to get off—off message, I mean."

"What about straight cock?" Michael asks. "I had this buddy back in college. He knew I was a suckslut, but he was cool with it. He said, just keep away from mine. He was hot. He buzzed his hair down to the skull. He always had his eyes squeezed slightly shut as if he were squinting in the sun. This guy enjoyed being looked at. He liked to cause a stir. Stroll buck naked down the hall from the shared showers with his towel over his shoulder. He'd stop and talk and absently play with his cock."

Hidden behind the lectern, Michael pokes the tip of his cock through his open fly. It's thick, pale, and too big for his grip. He brings up his hand, licks his palm, reaches down, and begins to stroke.

"So one day, we were strung out and drinking beers and watching the game in his dorm room. Just the two of us. Sox win, and he changed the channel to "Charlie's Angels." It was late, but I wasn't about to leave. There was something in the air. I had—have—a fine-tuned instinct for cock. Whenever or wherever it's likely to show its face. My friend peeled off his shirt and threw it at the dirty clothes hamper. He was lying there in just basketball shorts. His hand was beneath the waistband, his eyes on the TV. He yawned and mentioned how horny the Angels made him. All those hot girls. My mouth went dry. I wet my lip with my tongue. There was a rise in my crotch, just as he grabbed his. He had a huge erection; it tented his shorts—a circus big top. He still wasn't looking at me, but he pulled his basketball shorts down to midthigh. I licked down his shaft and pulled at the folds of his loose, fleshy sac. I bobbled the nuts with my tongue. He eased down and put his hand on my shoulder and said, 'Easy. Real slow.' So I licked and lapped and pulled a tube of piña colada-flavored gel from my pocket. It was my sixth dick that day; I figured I was due for some dessert. I squeezed out a dab and worked it into the stiff flesh with my fingers. When I went down again, he became quiet as death. His eyes were still closed. A light scrape of teeth made him tighten and go, 'Mmmmmm.' Sucking his cock was like choking up on the sweetest baseball bat in the world. Drool and lube matted his pubes. I tweaked his nipple with one hand. 'I'm gonna jizz,' he said. I pulled away and milked the shaft, staring at that eye at the tip, ready to catch the load that squirted free. His belly tightened, abs in stark relief. And then a thick chrism spilled down his shaft, like from a slow-flowing volcano. I caught gobs of the stuff in my hands and licked it warm off my fingers. He groaned quietly, and then immediately fell asleep. Man, he tasted so good, it made me want to cut off his shorts and run away with them so I'd have something to remember him by."

Affirmative grunts rise from the circle of men. Michael's dick throbs. The tip is sticky. The balls are drawn up in his sac. His mouth aches for something hard and fleshy. For a moment, he leaves off stroking.

"Not that I think that's a good thing," he says. His tone suggests the contrary: that it's a very good thing indeed.

"Michael," Gerry warns, "maybe you're not quite ready..."

Michael points at him. On Michael's finger, a flick of precum glints under the dim light. "I know what you're thinking, Gerry: this is too self-aggrandizing. Too much of me in the telling. But I'm the first to admit that I am not in the top ranks of sucksluts. The professionals. The kings."

Michael's accusing finger moves around the circle and comes to rest on a diminutive middle-aged man in a seersucker suit. "My modest friend Matt the Mouth, that's him there. From personal experience I can tell you it doesn't get any better. I bow down before him."

Michael inclines his head.

"Even at his age, he's unerring," says Michael. "A prodigious talent. He can size up a fellow at a hundred yards and rattle off the stats: cut/uncut, length, fast or slow, pubes trimmed or curly, teeth or no teeth, purple head, veiny, crooked—you name it, this guy can feed you the scoop. Some of it experience, but some of it a gift. 'Gotta be good at something,' Matt always says. Unfailingly humble. He always lets you have first choice. And he doesn't mind *sharing* a stray cock now and again. A real saint."

Men crane their heads to get a look at the object of Michael's praise. Michael shakes a knowing finger to temper their spirits.

"But my friends, whether you're Matt, or you're me, or you're you, you know as well as I do—it starts to get you in trouble. Cock will do that. You know how it goes."

"Say it, brother!"

"What was your rock bottom, Michael?" Gerry prompts. "Don't be afraid to share."

"Oh, man. Like when my boss stopped by my desk three days running, and each time I was in the men's room sucking off the new fresh-off-the-boat hottie janitor. Or when my doctor determined that—by volume—my daily diet consists of nine-tenths jizz. Or the fact that my tongue muscle is bigger than my biceps. And no ChapStick can ever soothe my calloused lips."

He opens his mouth. At the sight of that well-used maw, ready for action, a few flies unzip in a kind of Pavlovian reaction, as if Michael's mouth has gravity, capable of drawing cock to him from around the solar system. Sweat breaks out on Gerry's brow. His iron self-control begins to waver.

Michael continues: "Rock bottom? Once, during lesbian party week in P-town, I was so hard up for cock that I broke into a minivan and stole one poor dyke's entire stock of dildos. It took two or three of them in my mouth at a time just to tame the urge." He sighs. "It's a downward spiral. You swear off the cock. You bottom yourself silly, as if you could so easily switch your addiction to another orifice. But it always comes back to the swinging dick. The cock at three hundred yards. The hot lawn boy with the big package beneath his Daisy Duke cutoff jeans. The—"

All of a sudden, there's a commotion in the part of the circle farthest from the podium. Michael peers through the haze and smoke. Despite the three solid dickless years under his belt, there's Gerry, going at it on his neighbor's manmeat like a kid bobbing for apples at a Halloween party. Michael leaps from behind the lectern. Intent on saving Gerry from his own weakness, he bodily throws himself between Gerry and the object of his affection. Then he sees it: the rigid pole between muscular thighs, the dark pubes against the pale skin, the hip tattoo, and the cock's twitching dance as it searches for Gerry's electric tongue. Who could blame Gerry for falling from the wagon?

Michael kneels. Together, he and Gerry crush their faces into that crotch, licking balls, nibbling the base, one on either side. They share it; first Gerry, then Michael, tasting Gerry's saliva slicked all over the cock from head to tip. Gerry rubs the head of it on Michael's parted lips. The precum leaks and tastes of tears.

Another man sees Michael's cock through the open fly of his pants. He bends down and sucks and pulls at the flesh. In turn, another man finds the previous man's unused member. And on it goes, around the circle, each man helplessly drawn to the next cock over, until the whole meeting dissolves into a massive suckfest, man sucking off man sucking off man, like a chain of fleshy daisies. The proverbial wagon doesn't merely lose a few passengers; it overturns and crashes into a tree. A forest, really. A forest of flesh.

They slink away afterward, shamefaced, satiated, not a little

proud, sneaking quick sniffs of the ass-stink under their fingertips and drying their hands on their pant legs, backhanding
a sleeve across their mouths. Getting ready, no doubt, for the
rest of the dick in the street.

Michael and Gerry look at one another and sigh dejectedly.

"Accept what you cannot change," Michael intones. He
glances around at the folding chairs thrown aside, the floor lit-
tered with underwear, spent condoms, and gobs of lube.

"Have the courage to change what you can," Gerry answers
firmly. The two men pull up their pants and zip their flies and
inspect each other's chins for signs of drool.

FROM *PUSH*: WILLIAMSBURG SWIMMING POOL

Blair Mastbaum

I walk back down Metropolitan Avenue, a usually busy two-lane road that connects Williamsburg with the Brooklyn-Queens Expressway, toward the ice-clogged East River. The snow is coming down pretty hard, big flakes covering the street, the sidewalk, and the stoops of the tenements, making the whole world white. The road is dead now because of the blizzard, but it's usually jammed with trucks. One side of the street, the south side, on my left, is dark. The right side still has power. It's like viewing an art exhibit as I walk down the street, lights on one side, black on the other.

My ex-boyfriend Billy, who I'm still obsessed with, would appreciate it so much, but he's making out in front of some idiot's camera in some stupid sweaty hot bar.

I actually start to cry. I didn't feel it coming on, but the tears are running down my freezing cold cheeks. I feel more miserable than I ever have. I'm so cold and depressed that I think I'm actually turning numb, turning blank like a cutout of a human being. I wish I was made of plastic and cardboard. I'm too fucking sad to feel any longer. It's too hard to be *real*.

I stumble down to the corner of Metropolitan and Bedford avenues and find myself standing in front of an old indoor pool known as the Metropolitan Public Baths. It's basically an old natatorium, a square post office looking building with ornate columns and the name carved proudly overhead in the marble. The letter *U* in *public* looks like a *V* because it's supposed to look Greek or Roman I think. Everyone calls it the Williamsburg pool.

I walk up the front steps and look inside. It's dark except for some dim emergency exit lights and a yellowish floodlight shining on the entrance desk. As I lean on the door to look inside, it just falls open. It feels light as a feather even though it would be really heavy to a normal person, a person who's not numb and intensely sad at the same time.

It's really warm, like balmy tropical-island warm inside and the scent of the chlorine makes me feel safe, I guess because of the familiarity of it.

I was a high school swimmer and my swim team brothers, as we called ourselves, were my best friends, or as close to best friends as I had anyway.

Without them, I would have been even more alone and lonely through high school.

They thought I was weird and I refused to shave my legs for meets and give high fives to winners, but in the lanes of the swimming pool, we were just guppies swimming as fast as we could. You couldn't even tell us apart. That was comforting to me. And the swim team was super low profile, like most girls didn't even know the team existed, so I never had to act interested in some girl because there was never one around, period.

One of my swim brothers, the best swimmer on the team, a super-pale, blond Russian immigrant kid named Boris, was a homo.

Me and Boris would smoke pot after swim practice in his enormous room (he said his dad imported caviar to the U.S. market) and then we'd make out and possibly jerk off together, sometimes to a magazine he had of Eastern European boys in the mountains outside some amazing looking city that Boris said he'd been to but he couldn't remember the name.

It was thrilling and totally normal at the same time. We got used to seeing each other's dicks so much that seeing his— uncut, straight, medium sized, and really pale—was just like seeing his face in a way. It defined him. It was perfect really.

These stoned afternoons saved my childhood from eternal tedium.

It wasn't about the sex for me. Usually, my body was exhausted from swimming so hard and I'd have rather just listened to music and lain back on the carpet with a joint and talked about getting the fuck out of there, meaning small-town Oregon logging country mixed with hippie drum-circle types where we grew up, Corvallis to be precise. I liked how close we were those afternoons, surrounded by a hazy bubble of pot and hormones, the sweet-smelling warm air between us, or the occasional stench of the smoked trout that he liked to eat in the afternoons. I still like smoked trout a lot.

Anyway, Boris sort of demanded the kissing, and I didn't

object. He could make out forever and I got tired of it quickly but I could handle it.

I liked it, too, but really the reason I was there was because I didn't want to lose him to some other dude, to some other situation. I didn't love him and I never could have.

It's not like Boris wasn't cute. He looked like a wild animal in the way that only Eastern Europeans can. He had pasty white skin and yellow-white hair and he was six foot two with slender muscles and small nipples spaced a bit farther apart than most boys'.

He hardly spoke English, too, which was good. He said my name like *cut*.

I projected my idea of the perfect person onto him and he filled the part well—this spaced-out, always stoned, always horny Euro-type, with bloodshot eyes, field-mouse brown pubic hair, and always, some strange take on high fashion mixed with sports clothes that only Russians can get away with wearing. He had a T-shirt that read, SUPER MUSCLES RUNNER and he thought it looked cool, and on him, it did. I imagined him liking my favorite books, like the Joan Didion essays I was obsessed with at the time, and my favorite bands and artists.

A slow, horrible dropping feeling takes over in my stomach. I have to shove sixteen-year-old Boris and the lonely days of high school out of my brain.

Boris is probably married to a nice Estonian girl now. He probably remembers me as some weird homo.

I walk inside the pool building. It's still warm in here, which feels excellent. I walk past the wood-grain Formica entrance desk, where the sign-in sheet is still lying open in a blue binder, and into the actual pool room. It's pretty dark with just a thin sheen of grayish moonlight coming in the high, small windows that are shaped like half moons.

I take off my coat and set it on a chair, a plastic version of those chaise lounges they had on the *Titanic*. My arm is midnight blue in the almost darkness.

I sit down on the tile and feel the water with my feet. It's still womb warm. The electricity hasn't been off nearly long enough for the water to turn cold, or maybe it's heated with gas or oil.

I feel really loose and comfortable for the first time in weeks, maybe months. The only sound is a gentle trickle of tiny waves hitting the sides of the swimming pool. That, and the sound of my breathing. I might be able to hear my heartbeat, but I can't decide for sure. Oh, and there's this static in my ears, a whirring, like after you beat off and you're just sitting there in the silence with come on your stomach—that high-pitched white noise.

I slide off my shoes and socks and then unbutton my pants and slide them off. I stand up just wearing my boxer shorts. They're *Jaws II*-patterned, a great white depicted like it's coming out of the fly.

I slide down my boxer shorts and stand naked in the enormous room. It's a powerful feeling for some reason, maybe it's just the *I'm a boy and my dick is powerful* thing, but it feels more important somehow, like me standing here right now is part of something bigger.

I try to remember when I was last naked, with the exception of quickly getting in and out of the bath, barely catching a glimpse of my dick as I slide on my old robe. I haven't really been naked in months if not a year, and certainly not with another person.

I start to get a boner from thinking about nakedness, which feels good, but makes me aware I'm alone. My dick is calling out for someone, but the rest of me can't provide it.

I think of being a person I've never been before, someone who calls some dude up with the intention of hanging out and having sex and then saying good-bye, maybe I'll call you again if I'm bored.

It would be the biggest exception in my personality in the last five years at least. Maybe I should do it, but who would I call? I do what a lonely emo boy does best. I cup my balls with one hand and start to jerk off with the other one, as slow as I possibly can. At least I'll make this last awhile if I can't actually have a boy to smell and touch while I'm doing it. I lean back and close my eyes for a few strokes, and then I hear something—a scuff on the tile floor, just a filter of the heater switching on? I'm not sure. I stop, stand still, and listen.

I look toward the entry doors on the far side of the pool. It's too dark to really see anything, but as my eyes adjust, I see a still figure standing in the doorway facing me.

I flinch, grab and pull up my pants with fast, jerky motions. I realize I've forgotten my underwear, which is lying by my feet. I reach for my T-shirt, but before I can get it on, a male voice asks, "Who are you?"

"The door was open," I say, my voice quivering, as I kick my underwear under the chaise lounge. "I just came in here trying to get warm."

The figure moves across the room on the other side of the pool.

I can tell he's a dude, maybe in his twenties, skinny, but I can't tell anything else about him because it's too dark.

I hear the rustling sound of clothes coming off, then the

metal clink of a belt buckle hitting the tile floor, and the soft sound of underwear falling down legs, and then a gentle dive into the water.

The boy comes up, takes a deep breath, and almost grunts, or moans—like the water feels good, refreshing, or warm or comfortable in some way.

I start to sort of buzz inside, my heart rate rising. I just stand here still, shirtless, shocked. The concept that this could turn out to be somewhat interesting or sexy begins to barely enter my brain. My boner comes back, this time restrained by my pants.

"Get in the water," the guy says.

I don't think. I just react. I jump in wearing my pants, only half buttoned up, with my T-shirt balled up in my clenched hand.

The water is so warm all my shivers from the entire winter melt away. I've never been so warm, so thrilled. My blood starts flowing faster. I piss without even noticing for the first couple of seconds. I float on my back, secure and cradled by the warm chlorinated water.

The boy swims over near me, treading water. I can see now that he has floppy, dark, almost black hair; he's skinny and cute, goofy looking in an unpredictable way, sort of ghoulish. He smells like musk, a little like a horse and a bushel of barley, a good round boyish smell, mixed with the chlorine.

I finally gather enough courage in my tight little inexperienced body to swim right up to him. What I see first is a pierced lip—sort of sexy, sort of tragic, a bit trashy.

"What are you doing here?" the boy asks.

"I just wandered in," I say. "It was so cold outside. I was alone. I just tried the door and it was open." I wrap my arms around him, bony shoulders, warm back.

He looks at me like he's analyzing my face, so I close my eyes. "At first, I thought you were this guy Theo. He had a Mohawk, a real one, not a sort-of one. But when he took his boxers off, he didn't have pubic hair. It was gross."

"I have pubic hair," I say without thinking. Plus, I'm pretty drunk really.

He smiles and pushes me underwater. My face goes under and I accidentally suck in some water and come up coughing, my throat a scratchy mess. He's a fucking killer, the Brooklyn Drowner. "Fuck, I almost drowned," I say, coughing.

He swims across the pool and treads water in the deep end.

I swim over to him, fast, direct and without considering every possible scenario, a cycle I get caught up in too much and something I have pledged to stop doing.

He reaches down into my wet pants and holds on to my boner. He slides down my pants and starts to jack me off. It feels better than good, like falling from a plane with no parachute, on opium—just perfect.

I reach down to his dick, too, which is hard, really hard. I jerk him off a little and kiss him hard on the mouth, causing my teeth to cut his lip slightly and I taste the iron of his water-diluted blood.

Blood mixes with our spit and it tastes so much like boy that I get even more turned on, more than in months. We make out and come in two minutes flat. I scream as I'm coming. I scream and grunt and shoot into the warm water and it's the best feeling I've had since me and my ex-boyfriend Billy met and found a forest grove in Central Park and sucked each other off and came in each other's mouths. It was close to that.

I hear a snowplow truck drive past outside. The snow is still coming down.

Our sperm floats across the surface of the still swimming pool.

"What's your name?"

He hangs from the diving board with his arms, pulling himself up with backward pull-ups. When he raises himself up, I see that his dick is still half-hard, getting softer.

"Scooby."

"Cool," I say, not thinking and still a little out of breath.

"I want to die of a heroin overdose," he says.

"I don't have any, but I do have some whiskey." I get out of the pool, freezing cold, and run to get my bottle of whiskey. I pick it up and realize that I've already drunk three-fourths of it as I almost fall running back to the warmth of the swimming pool water.

A loud metal clang echoes through the echoey pool room.

"Who's in there?" a loud, masculine, New York accented voice calls out.

We both try to be as still as we can, but my heart is beating like crazy and my hands are shaking, causing a tiny tsunami across the surface of the water.

Not only am I trespassing, I'm naked in a swimming pool with a boy I don't know during a blizzard and a blackout. This is not going to look good.

Keys jangling, flashlights searching like invasive alien eyes, two cops walk like robo-cops into the pool room, like they know exactly what they're going to find—some stupid, horny, depressed, art homos—and they don't care for the type. I don't care for the type and I'm sitting here being it. It's a truly pathetic moment in my life. I scan the dark room for my underwear and remember that my pants are lying in a wet, heavy pile on the tile.

I'm going to jail without pants on.

I jump out of the pool and grab my boxer shorts and step into them as fast as I can. I slip with only one leg in and fall on my side, trying to catch myself with my hand. It hurts like hell. I think I sprained my wrist.

"Just remain still!" one the cops yells.

I sit down and let the pain cycle through my arm and then I slide my other leg into my underwear.

The cop shines the flashlight on me just soon enough to catch a view of my dick as I slide my underwear up. "Get dressed!" He turns his back and waits for me to get dressed.

The other cop, a woman I think, judging by the silhouette, walks back out into the lobby and through another door, talking on her CB the whole time.

Scooby gets out of the water and walks to the opposite side of the pool to get his clothes, which are all black: skinny jeans and a T-shirt with an old photo of Dennis Cooper on it.

Just as he's about to pull his T-shirt back on, the lights flip on, brighter than I ever would have thought they'd be, bright as a stadium at night.

The humiliating thing that the light brings about is that I don't mind looking at the cop. The gaze I want to avoid is that of Scooby, the stranger whose dick I was just touching. I've never done this before and I feel shallower than a mud puddle. I feel like a slimy, bourgeois loser; a stupid asshole led by his balls, controlled not by his intellect, but by his sperm, which is desperately trying to escape this depressed, underfed body. It's truly pathetic.

The woman cop walks back out to the swimming pool, hiding a smile, and the other cop gets out his handcuffs.

"Okay, hands behind your backs."

I look at Scooby to see what he does and he just stands there, not acting like anything. I hate him.

He's not offering to help me, not even looking my way. He's checking a fucking Blackberry, typing those stupid little keys with his thumbs.

Luckily, this pisses the female cop off, too, so she practically runs over to him and cuffs him.

The two cops take us out and put us into the backseats of separate cars.

I'm in a fucking police car, freezing cold with only wet boxer shorts and a winter coat on. I can see my dick through the thin, wet, white fabric. This is the worst possible place I could be on the entire earth right now. This makes me more depressed, more sad, than I've ever felt before. I begin to sob. I'll go to jail with no pants on. I'll have to call my ex-boyfriend to bail me out. I'll be pathetic once again. Even the memory of this night in the abandoned pool, something I would have jacked off imagining, will be tainted with darkness, with failure, like the rest of my life.

DAMAGED

David May

*Fantasy is toxic: the private cruelty
and the world war both have their
start in the human brain.*
　　　　　　—Elizabeth Bowen

It was generally agreed that the initial impact of
the bus's side-view mirror hadn't caused Kevin's temporary loss of memory, but rather the
second blow to the head from when he landed
on the sidewalk. The first only caused the con-
cussion; it was the cracking of his head on the
cement that knocked years from his memory.
Which collision (either with concrete or with
stainless steel) would have the profoundest affect on Kevin's future by impairing any ability
to experience his former passions, would never
be known for certain.

Kevin woke up in the hospital and knew at once where he was, and that he must have been in an accident of some kind for him to be getting a sponge bath while heavily bandaged and aching all over—even if he had no memory of the Chicago Transit Authority's assault, nor of how his head had ricocheted from one hard surface to the next; or even of how he had spent the last few days. It was only when he saw Lee standing at the foot of the bed that Kevin showed anything approaching confusion.

"Who are you?"

"I'm Lee. We live together. We had a wedding last summer in my parents' backyard. Remember?"

"No. Are you trying to put one over on me?"

Lee pulled out his wallet and showed Kevin the picture of the two of them holding hands, both in morning suits, in a suburban backyard.

"For real?" was Kevin's only response.

Doctors were called, questions asked of Kevin, questions to which he no longer knew the answers: *What year was it? Who was the president of the United States? What was his address?*

Looking at his driver's license, Kevin saw that, indeed, it was the same address as the one on Lee's license. He was also surprised to see that his hairline had receded and that he'd grown a beard.

No, I haven't given you the expected descriptions of their godlike beauty, chiseled features, huge cocks and perfect bodies. This is because these details are irrelevant to the tale being told—as well as being untrue. But you, the Common Reader, want to know these things; you want to be assured that the

*men you're imagining are worth getting hard for, worth think-
ing about as you rearrange your crotch. Suffice it to say that
Kevin is fair and Irish while Lee is dark and of Welsh de-
scent, and that they had, until this moment, shared that peculiar Celtic sensibility of taking a joy in life (which is to say,
in food, music, the telling of tales, dancing and making love)
with a passion normally associated with Mediterranean peo-
ples, while living as a northern race. Both are furry and over
thirty, though Lee is a few years senior. They are burly men
who work out together several days a week, and if they were
the type of men one was looking for online, one would call
them Muscle Bears. Their beards might change with the sea-
sons and the fashions, but they are always bearded and know
that they are the kind of men who are the handsomer for it.*

"Sometimes these things happen," offered the nurse, a small
brown woman with an indeterminate accent. "Memories usually come back in a few days. Do you want to see your mother
now, Kevin? She's waiting outside."

"Hell no! If that bitch is here, you better call security because she is not supposed to be anywhere near me. There's
a restraining order!" Kevin turned to Lee for confirmation.
"That's still true, isn't it?"

"Yup. And it goes for both of us."

"But she's your mother..."

"She also arranged to have me kidnapped so I could be
held captive by some charlatan who promised he'd make me
straight—but only after he'd taken all of her money, of course.
Ask her yourself, if you want to. She'll be happy to tell you
about her Christian duty."

"If you don't call security, I will," added Lee firmly.

The nurse hesitated, once more offering the information that the woman sitting in the hall with her well-worn Bible was Kevin's mother, so Lee reached for the phone as the nurse shook her head in disbelief. A few minutes later Kevin's mother could be heard screaming in the hallway: threats of legal action, God's wrath, and the newspapers being informed of this outrage were all proffered with no effect. Lee smiled to hear the theatrically maternal cries of moral outrage, then turned back to Kevin expecting to see the same smug satisfaction on his partner's face, but saw instead two empty eyes that registered no satisfaction in once again frustrating his mother's martyrdom, but rather a dull dismay at the depth of the disturbed woman's emotion.

Friends came to visit Kevin in the hospital. Photo albums and mementoes were proffered. Stories were told of Kevin and Lee's life together. Bit by bit memories were recovered and Kevin's lost years were pieced together. His college years, his courtship with Lee, his teaching second grade in Highland Park, all came back, but elicited no feeling from him. Always passionate about food, with very particular likes and dislikes, he now ate whatever was put before him when he was hungry, and then lost interest in eating when his stomach no longer felt empty. Always fond of children and animals, the mere thought of either now made him anxious and uneasy. His shared passion with Lee (fucking first thing in the morning and the last thing at night with the addition, when possible, of matinees and predinner romps), that had been the envy of all, was now like a withered ear of corn, a dried husk with no fruit within. Television provided no diversion in the hospital, offering only noise and confusing images; even his favorite old movies meant nothing to him.

When he came home, Kevin turned to books, the ones he had loved since he was a child growing up in southern Illinois. He started with the *Oz* books, once forbidden to him by his parents (and so, as a child, read only at the library), the complete collection of which were now his pride and joy.

The books he brought home had been examined with suspicion by his parents. No fairy tales, science fiction or fantasy, were allowed. Encyclopedia Brown, Tornado Jones, Henry Huggins and the Hardy Boys were grudgingly approved. Later came Laura Ingalls Wilder, Louisa May Alcott, Jack London and Mark Twain, and finally his favorite, Charles Dickens, all of them passing before his parents' ever persistent scrutiny. The Chronicles of Prydain and Narnia, along with Ray Bradbury's books and J.R.R. Tolkien's tomes, he hid in his school locker, only reading them in the homes of friends.

With sudden regularity, one or both of his parents would burst into his bedroom, accusation livid in their eyes as they pulled whatever he was reading from his hands, followed by their sullen disappointment at finding neither pornography nor self-abuse under their roof—both of which Kevin sensibly confined to deserted barns with his equally frustrated friends. Staying a few steps ahead of his parents, he took an easy pleasure in their bewilderment.

Now he read again the books he remembered loving, and in the comfort of familiar fiction he experienced something approaching pleasure. As the tales unraveled, as the characters' lives evolved through each story, he found a singular solace in the otherwise empty universe he had come to inhabit. Sex with Lee had become mechanical and only about orgasm, one more task to be completed. Only when he was fucked did he find some lasting pleasure; the complex chemistry of his lover's cum becoming a permanent part of him elevated his mood, sent into his bloodstream an endorphin-like release from an existence that was otherwise without affect. Alone in bed and dripping semen as his husband showered, he felt something like satisfaction: only then did he smile.

Unable to work, Kevin spent his days visiting psychiatrists, neurologists, social workers, attorneys, numerous therapists, the offices of his former union, and numerous government agencies in order to secure the needed income. Somewhere amidst his daily travels between and around Lake View and the Loop, it occurred to him that he could go to the baths. There he could again be fucked and again (since intimacy played no part in the primal joy that came from it) feel the same completion. Though he and Lee had until then been nominally monogamous, he paid his membership and went in without a second thought. The halls were not as crowded as he'd hoped, but there were enough men (and he was not so choosy about them, any more than he was about his diet) to provide the needed injection of cum; with more cum came more of the required chemistry. He felt better, almost happy, but ached for the euphoria he remembered once feeling in Lee's arms, legs, cock and buttocks.

It was also in the baths that he rediscovered pornography and found that the visual of other men fucking was comforting as well as arousing, and the lack of plot a requisite for his being able to concentrate on what he watched. In the pornography he found online he discovered what he most wanted to see: a single man being fucked by many men until he dripped semen, a beatific smile across the bottom's face. To be like that man, to be the man more men would want to leave their seed in, he took a renewed interest in his own appearance. He cut his hair short and trimmed his beard to little more than stubble. Now much thinner, he returned to the gym and firmed the farm-trained musculature waiting beneath his formerly *zaftig* frame. Almost every day he douched and went to one of the local bathhouses, got fucked and felt better. If Kevin was absent when Lee came home from work, Lee made his own dinner, walked the dog, and was happy to see Kevin looking so much better when he eventually came home with vague tales of losing track of the time. Lee was even happier to find Kevin was now eager for sex, or at least to get fucked, for only then was there any tenderness between them.

Until Lee woke up one morning with the clap, that is. At that moment everything Lee had suspected but denied came together with one final furious wave. He screamed at Kevin, whose impassive face drove him to distraction, yelled accusations that were only acknowledged with nods of agreement. Kevin denied nothing for he felt no remorse for his actions, but was, in fact, more intrigued than worried by Lee's outrage. It was not until Lee's hurt drove him to strike Kevin hard across the face in some final retaliation that Kevin felt anything at all. Pain, he realized at that moment, led to a pleasant release in its subsiding. If the pain were greater, so would be the subsequent release from it: just as every action had a reaction, so pain led to pleasure.

Frustrated at Kevin's lack of response, Lee stormed out and Kevin calmly went online looking for an apartment. By the time Lee returned to their condominium (looking over downtown Chicago because lake views were static, even dull, to their shared Celtic aesthetic), Kevin had packed what he deemed necessary and left, moving into a shabby little apartment a block off of Halsted Street. He now had the settlement from his accident and his disability checks to live on. Still able to feel guilt, or at least discomfort, at having caused Lee such distress (though not enough to make any amends to his husband, only enough to remove himself from Lee's proximity and so avoid further outbursts), he left a note bequeathing the condo to Lee. He moved out feeling something like satisfaction, partly because guilt had compelled him to make the gesture to the one who had been so kind to him, and partly due to his desire to be free of any future obligations now that they had used part of the settlement to pay the balance of their mortgage.

The apartment (damp and in need of painting, stinking of stale cooking smells and some faint chemical residue), recently abandoned by some disreputable character, hadn't been cleaned between tenants. In his cursory examination of the shelves and cupboards Kevin found a loaded gun that he left untouched, comforted by the presence of something so passive and yet so powerful in his meager home. Cheaply as he could he bought a bed big enough to be fucked in and whatever furniture and other household goods—the bare minimum—he needed to eat and read and live. His favorite books were piled against the walls of his bedroom. A laptop that played his pornographic DVDs sat on the kitchen table, always on, always connected to the world of men looking for a man like Kevin who was eager to take their seed, alerting Kevin to their calls as he read and reread the Brontës, Dickens, Austen, Thackeray, Trollope, James, Hardy and Woolf.

He was treated for the clap, tested for syphilis, but did not stop getting fucked. He refused any other intervention, so focused was he on the only physical relief he'd found to the static colorlessness of his life. Knowing that the addition of pain would increase his relief from the stolid gray blandness, Kevin haunted the leather bars and their back rooms dressed as he had seen his pornographic role models dressed, in chaps and vest. Now men beat his ass with a gloved hand or belt, twisted his nipples, held him by the throat long enough to instill, in his faint appreciation of such things, the hope for annihilation. He was never so close to feeling happy as when he returned to his dingy apartment just before dawn, bruised and aching, his ass dripping blood and cum. On these mornings, in those few seconds before drifting off to sleep, he felt content, even at peace.

It was, of course, only a matter of time before Lee found him, either by plan or by chance. Those who knew them saw Kevin in his new haunts, places where Lee would never go, and word eventually reached Lee of where Kevin could be found, and of what he was doing there. Lee's appearance at the Eagle that night was like the Bad Fairy's at Sleeping Beauty's christening: noisy, distressing and very unwelcome. He grabbed Kevin by the locked chain around his throat, swore at him, cursed him, spat in his face, and finally struck him hard enough to knock Kevin against the wall with such force that the impact echoed through the bar, causing a momentary pause in the otherwise constant buzz of conversation. No one intervened, of course, Kevin's reputation being such that bystanders assumed it was all part of a planned and negotiated scene: the deep, demented psychodrama of formerly reputable homosexuals who had recently eschewed bourgeois respectability. But when Kevin was slammed against the wall with that loud and distressing thud, it was his head that hit it first. Then something extraordinary happened.

Yes, I am a notorious romantic and will, as usual, provide you, the Common Reader, with a happy ending. But please remember that this is fiction. In doing my research for this romance of erotic possibilities, I learned that while much is known about the brain and how it functions after an injury, there is still more not known than known. Think of this story, then, as a black-and-white movie made Before the War, one wherein the writer projects his deepest desire into an otherwise disturbing tale. Experts might roll their eyes at the coming conclusion, but even they are compelled to admit that not enough is known to absolutely refute my fable of love challenged. And even if they can refute it, why should they want to when suspended disbelief is so essential to the enjoyment of any erotica?

Kevin wept. Everything unfelt for the past year suddenly gushed forward with tears, sobs and broken sentences: a confusion of joy and pain, of angst and pleasure, that fell into a single proverbial pile at the core of his being, a muddled mess of emotions, all fragments with jagged edges. Knowing that Kevin was constitutionally unable to fake tears, Lee gathered his husband in his arms, held him close, and took him outside into the cool autumn air. Eventually Lee loaded him into their car, secured him in his seat, and took him back to their condo with the downtown view. By the time they were in the elevator, Kevin was better able to stifle his sobs, but this meager control was lost when he saw the dog's excitement on seeing the return of his long lost friend. They went straight to bed. Lee held Kevin all night, even after the sobs subsided. Eventually they slept, the dog snoring quietly at their feet.

When they awoke it was not like it was before the accident. It never could or would be the same again. Something had returned, however, some vital fragment fallen back into place, and they awoke making love for the first time in over a year. Kevin was eager to please Lee in any way he could, remembering again the inner map of Lee's flesh and the secret soft places that made Lee writhe under Kevin's touch.

May I not do what I wish with my characters—even if their actions horrify the Common Reader? I know the inner workings of these men better than you do, and I am compelled to proceed to the coming finish—pun intended. I can't help it if you're yearning for some simple one-handed tale (many of which I'm not ashamed to have written) that relies on the formula recurrent to every gay skin magazine: ten pages, with sex on the first page, an upbeat ending. No, this tale must wend its way to its own conclusion, one that might be other than what the Common Reader prefers. And now I have to ask you to remember that Thanatos and Eros were not mere gods to the ancient Greeks, but Primal Forces and, more significantly, Inseparable from Birth: where one found One, one also found the Other, like Cosmic Conjoined Twins.

Kevin's tongue found Lee's asshole, found the moist smoothness beckoning beyond the otherwise hairy mounds of inviting flesh. The hole, unbreached for so long, resisted his ministrations at first, and it was only with patience and persistence that he caused the beige flower to open and give in to the onslaught it craved. Kevin's cock, truly tumescent for the first time since the accident, glistened with precum and spit as it found the familiar hole, the place where it had once been so welcome. As Kevin entered Lee, they looked into each other's eyes for confirmation:

Yes, I want you and all that you are.

No, we can never be separated again.

Yes, what you have I must have too.

No, I do not want to live without you so take me with you when you die.

Kevin passed the first sphincter and gasped with pleasure. Lee sharply inhaled, so unused was he now to the girth of Kevin's (or any other) cock. Kevin watched Lee's face until he saw it relax, then pulled out an inch before moving forward another two. Lee's body tensed, but did not for a moment recoil. Sweat poured off both their bodies even though they had hardly begun to fuck, their bodies trembling with shared anticipation. Their excitement was as mutual as the coming sacrament was necessary.

Now Kevin moved with more deliberation, in, then out, finding those centers of pleasure inside Lee's velvety fuckhole. Kevin watched Lee's face, the beatific grin, the angelic composure as Kevin's rhythm doubled. Kevin could not hold off very long. He was too excited, too eager, too in love.

"Are you sure?" he gasped between strokes.

"Yes!"

"This is what you want?"

"Yes!"

"It's not too late, I can still…"

But Lee grabbed Kevin's face and kissed him hard, sent his tongue down Kevin's throat. He knew the kiss would send Kevin over the edge and into oblivion. Then came the gushing of cum, the unleashing fury of so much unspent lust, of so much unspilled seed. Kevin's breaths came in short gasps. His body convulsed. He collapsed into his lover's arms and continued their kiss. When their mouths finally released each other, they looked again into each other's eyes. There would be no going back now. The sacrament was almost complete.

Lee rolled Kevin over onto the bed, onto the sweat-soaked spot he had just occupied. He turned Kevin over onto his stomach and shoved his cock inside him without so much as spit. His cock was bigger than Kevin's so it hurt all the more. The assault drew blood, but both knew that it must, that Lee must have his due now, that Kevin must be punished. Lee pounded into Kevin, cursing him the whole while, uttering words he'd never have spoken before to one he loved beyond words:

"Fucking bitch whore!"

"Yes!"

"Son of a bitch bastard slut!"

"Yes!"

"Fucking skank cum bucket!"

"Yes!"

Lee smacked Kevin's ass hard with his open hands, again, and again, until he felt his palms sting.

"Cocksucking faggot!"

"Yes!"

"Fucking cesspool!"

"Yes!"

Lee held off longer than Kevin had been able to. He wanted to prolong the punishment to add to the injury he was inflicting on the one he so desperately needed. He lay right on top of Kevin, wrapping an arm around Kevin's throat, tightening the grip as he came closer to cumming, choking Kevin when he did cum in great gushes, not knowing for sure (but suspecting, even hoping) that Kevin blacked out as Lee spilled so much seed deep inside him.

Later that day they went to the dingy little apartment off of Halsted Street to collect Kevin's books, clothes and laptop. Kevin remembered the gun (still loaded, still untouched), and checking with a quick glance that it was still there, was glad to firmly shut the door on it and the comfort it had once threatened.

Lee and Kevin stayed together, but things were never the same, for they were no longer the same men. Their shared intellectual life returned to its former richness as long as it was limited to books, plays and films that Kevin was familiar with before the accident—fortunately this provided a nearly inexhaustible resource.

Kevin still floundered at times, unable to find the right words, confused at the depth of others' emotions, unsure of what task next needed doing. He felt his emotions profoundly now, but with the same depth and certainty as the dog felt his, uncomplicated by contradicting passions or subtle colorations. Often confused, and always rudderless, he followed the orders Lee left for him each morning lest Kevin slip back into the habit of spending his days cruising online:

> Vacuum and dust after you walk the dog.
> Then scrub the bathroom until it sparkles. Go to the
> gym and remember to eat lunch. Play outside with
> the dog in the afternoon. Bring in the mail. Make
> dinner. Be prepared for punishment.

Kevin obeyed, and like the dog, was happiest in obedience. He accepted punishment with pleasure for he knew from whence it came, and how much he needed Lee to feel whole. They rarely spoke of their new arrangement, only accepted it and the joy it brought them. They did not clothe it in leather and perform for the common crowd, nor did they name it. It simply was, and that was enough for both of them.

Lee was once more content, albeit in a different way than he had been before the accident. He felt his hands were full with two dogs now instead of just one—even if one of them read and walked on two feet. He loved Kevin with a firm hand as much as with a hard cock and willing hole. They made love as often as they had before, though how they made it had changed remarkably, and Kevin anticipated his punishments as eagerly as the dog did his walks. When friends or family saw the new depth of Kevin's devotion to Lee (so doglike that it made many uncomfortable), they asked how the two were getting on, expecting some innocuous answer. Lee was always the one to respond:

"We've reached an acceptable level of dysfunction."

Everyone sensed it was better not to ask for more details than that.

REMEMBERED MEN

Shane Allison

He was younger than me. He lived in a housing project. He had strawberry-blond hair with pubes to match. His ass was firm in dark blue shorts. He had kissable lips. He was an asshole all grown up. He had more foreskin than you could shake a stick at. He had a pretty big dick for someone his size. He had buck teeth. He was poor white trash who gave great head. He had an ass like a football player. He was such a nerd. He asked me to take a photo of my dick and bring it to school. He worked as an usher at a movie theatre. He liked to get fist-fucked. He sucked me off at a urinal. His brother was also gay. He wanted me to prove that I loved him by swallowing it. He fucked me senseless. His name was Tony. He was my first. He had the worst case of dandruff. He was too damn skinny for my tastes. He had man-breasts. He had a short, fat, pretty prick. He nibbled my earlobes. He taught Spanish at the local university. His cat licked the hair grease from my head as its master rode me like a bull. His cat licked his balls from behind as his master sucked me. He came on my stomach. He parted my asscheeks. He fingered my ass with his married finger. It hurt a little, but after the initial pain, it felt pretty damn good. His dick came up to his belly button. His last name was *Cocke*. He answered the door wearing nothing but green shorts and a durag. He slapped me around and I liked it. He swallowed my cum. He made me suck his balls. He made me suck his nipples. He called me a whore. He's right. He called me a whore and I loved him even more. He stood me up. He shoved a sex toy up in me. His dick was pierced. He had a British accent. He said, "Get down there and suck it." He wore latex underwear. He never did call the next day like he said he would. He wouldn't stop calling. He started to freak me out when he came by unexpectedly. He asked, "Are you ready for the rim chair?" He was old and balding. He was fat and just right. He was a tad too sissyish for my blood. He had blushing balls in a leather cock ring. He told me I could move in if I drank his piss. He asked, "You want to be my pig boy?" He kept saying, "Let me in you." He spoke with the thickest New York accent. He lived in Jersey. He was a rough punk with tattoos. He was blond and bearded. He had three dogs. He and I drank coconut rum and talked about "Queer as Folk." His breath smelled of fish and cigarettes. He said, "I hope you're not getting drunk just to have sex with me." He was Italian and talked too much. He had hard thighs. He had filthy fingernails. He was Jewish, you know. He picked fights with me.

He took the piercing out of his dick. He was much cuter with the Afro. He was HIV positive. His family had no idea. He talked dirty to me. He was called a fag by bullies and high school football players. He was happily married. He swore to me he was disease free. His wife hadn't a clue. His milk-white skin. He was moving to Europe. He told me why, but I forgot. He handcuffed me. He used the whip to take his frustrations out on my flesh. He asked, "Are you a homosexual?" He told me to take off my pants. He held me at knifepoint. He busted us both for lewdness down by the tracks. He was a cop undercover. He was Greek and new to the city. He was old-fashioned. He had a white girlfriend. He was Puerto Rican. He claimed he liked the flowers. He had soft, red fur around his asshole. He walked me home out of the rain. His cigarette breath on my neck. He asked as I began to finger-fuck his ass, "Can I go to the bathroom before you do that?" He snored and belched. He farted in my face as we sixty-nined each other. He said, "For ten dollars I'll suck it right off the bone." He said he wasn't a hustler, but just wanted money for something to eat. He sucked me off for two bucks. He told me he wasn't homeless or a drug addict. He blew me right there on the hood of his car. He worked at a gas station. His face and back was burned. He drove an old Jaguar. He fucked me like I had a pussy. He said, "I appreciate the cards and love letters." He said I came on too strong. He accused me of keying his car. He was so heavy on top of me, I couldn't breathe. His apartment had hardwood floors. His bed with the pale-blue sheets. His roommate was asleep in the next room, but he didn't care. He told me to keep quiet. He asked, "Do you think your roommates would like to join in?" He drove naked through the dirt roads. He had come three times already.

He was such a pig. He asked, "Would you like me to drink your piss now?" He called me Shawn. He wore black shoes with buckles. His jeans and underwear pulled down around his ankles. He left his stall door open for all to see. He told me to clean up my cum. He asked me if I was black. He thought I was West Indian. His shirt with yellow armpit stains. He had low-hanging balls. His dimpled bubble-butt. His moustache pricked my lip. He left me sore for days. His flat feet, the bony toes. His braids all in rows. His yellow bandana. His filthy asscrack. His hairy ass in the denim chaps. His hot, Hispanic accent. His Mohawk haircut. His polished fingernails. His pierced lips around my dick. He asked me what I was into. His mouth filled with all that cum and spit. He stood me up. He avoided me in the hall. He ignored my calls. He said he didn't care about looks. His toes were pretty and pedicured. He lived in Soho. He was a geology major. He loved Steven Spielberg. He was eight years older than me. He freaked me out with his obsession for teenage boys. He worked at a bowling alley. He looked like Madonna from the *Papa Don't Preach* video. He wore a fake carnation in his hair. His head was shaved. His crotch was shaved. He was on the down low. His parents didn't know. He tinted the windows of his car so he could make out with guys in parking lots. His dirty socks thrown in the corner of the room. He had a mole on his dick. He drank too much. He was a filthy, sexist bastard. He warned me about the cops in this place. His dick with all those veins. He had all that built-up dickcheese. He liked to wear makeup. He won a glow-in-the-dark rubber in a bingo game. He was a motivational speaker who lived in the Bronx. He performed as a drag queen at a club I forget the name of. He was a pretty-eyed tranny. He dressed better than most of the women

I know. He stepped out wearing a black miniskirt. He had a mullet and smelled of cheap perfume. He was bisexual. He was a drunken old queen wearing a fake fur. He was a heathen. He was a born-again Christian. He was a gay Republican. He was torn between his religion and his love for men. He was such a club kid. He was such a pretty boy. He couldn't come for doing so much coke. He paid top dollar for my soiled undies. He wanted to fuck right there in the hallway. He lived with his ailing mother. He said, "Damn you're huge." He took long whiffs of my socks. He held the poppers to my nose. He was butt-naked in the park. He fought with the drunken guy whose wallet was stolen at the Unicorn. He said, "Easy with the teeth, dude." He said, "C'mon, I'm trying to suck a dick here." He had muscles like you would not believe. He liked getting spanked. He looked like a young Jeff Daniels. He had untrustworthy eyes. He made the best vodka breezes in the West Village. His shimmering torso. He just stood there jacking off. He threw up on my dick. He gave me a soapy rag for the mess. He liked the poem I wrote. He slapped my ass with his dick. He was a Brooklyn thug. He asked if I had any weed on me. He was an Irish chef. He had to leave the club early. He said he had to go to church the next day. He had popsicle-red lips. His pink piss slit. He gave me herpes. He said, "Maybe you should start dating girls." He sucked the scat right off my dick. He cheated on his wife with me and from the looks of her, who could blame him? His name was Melvin. His dick was the first I ever sucked. He looked like Jerry Springer, but better looking. He had a dog named Byron. He was too drunk to fuck. He told me my dick was beautiful. He turned me into a size queen. He scared the hell out of us. He asked if he could join in when he caught us fucking. He said I smelled like good weed. He was this cute, Middle Eastern boy. He offered me some Jack Daniels. He left me chafed and scabbed, but I liked it. He cruised truck stops for dick. He had a baby dick. His dick was cold, but it warmed up quite nicely in my mouth. He lived for the tearooms. He liked to bite and pinch. He reminded me of all that great sex I used to have in the park. He pissed in the booths. He kicked me out and yelled, "Faggot ass!" He had hepatitis C. His cum tasted kind of Cloroxy. He said it wouldn't hurt if I just relaxed. He said, "You gotta come, man, my legs are giving out." He turned his hat backward before he started to suck me. His dick smelled bad. His name was Jonathan. He jerked off in the mayonnaise at Burger King. He wore a black shirt that said SECURITY on the back. He broke up the sex orgy. He was a rugged trucker. He said if he didn't suck a dick soon, he'd explode. He squirted and came. He wore snakeskin boots that night. He was free on Mondays and Wednesday evenings. He wanted to come on my face. He almost came in my eye. He made me come without even touching me. He asked me what I was into. He was so naïve. He said he wasn't that big. He unzipped his pants and took it out. He was right. He wasn't that big. He was really *going to town* on his dick. He said, "I love the color of your skin." He adored the taste of unclean foreskin. He said, "Now suck it, slut!" He didn't like to be watched. He said, "Go away, nigger," when I stuck my dick under his stall. He lay in white sand sunbathing in the nude. He used a dirty sock to wipe up the mess. He said, "C'mon on, man. Glide me in." He said, "You wanna buttfuck me?" He didn't want to meet at his place due to the nosey neighbors. He fucked me in a cemetery. He bent over the bed of the truck and spread his asscheeks for me. His web name is Sexy Bear Butt. He wore a platinum blonde beehive wig. He'd only experimented with guys a few times. He and I had phone sex. He hung up as soon as I came. He said he loved me and I believed it. His name was Chris. His girlfriend found out about us. He was so big, he made me gag. He got pissed when I refused to swallow it. He laughed when I told him I had a crush on him. He shook his ass harder when I waved a dollar in his face. He drove a beat-up old Chevy. He came all over my maroon sweater. He drove a green Camaro. He threw my love letters away. He patted me on the head when I swallowed his cum. His breath was a mixture of peppermint and fish. He used to be a woman. He took me to Woodstock for the weekend. He had one ball, but a big, thick dick. He was my sugar daddy. He loved to get gangbanged. He tied me up. He gagged me with his stinking underwear. He was all the rage at the bathhouses. He believed in monogamy. He was a nelly bottom. He liked it rough. He sucked us both off. He said it felt good when his wife used a dildo. He found the Polaroids of my dick in a folder. He was such a sissy slut. He was a teddy bear bottom. He told me that my dick was a perfect fit. He'd always fantasized about what sex would be like with a black guy. He tugged my balls too hard. He liked how gentle I was. He wasn't into white guys. He cheated on his wife. His greasy anal plugs. He wore panties under his jeans. His girlfriend had no idea. He cock blocked me from the other boys. He said, "I keep my ass clean and love to get eaten." He preferred to rim a dirty asshole. He sucked me off on a stack of corn in the storage room where we used to be movie ushers. He had that one gold tooth in the front. He said, "You shot a big load." He confessed that his accent was fake and that he was really from Georgia. He struggled to stuff his dick in me all night long, but never got it in. He said I was tight. He got fucked by some guy he didn't know. He liked it bareback. He wanted me to come in his ass. He said, "Don't nut in my mouth." He drank my cum like it was beer. He kept saying, "Fuck me like I fuck my wife." He couldn't give head for shit to be such a slut. His ass smelled like Irish Spring. He ate me out for countless hours. He was able to fit two dicks up his ass at once. He said, "Let me see those titties." He wanted to sniff my feet while he jacked off. He left an imprint of his asscheeks on the dashboard of my truck. He said, "Too sweaty, dude, too sweaty." (Meaning my butt.) He was a famous poet. He said my underwear wasn't ripe enough. He yelled, "Fuck my white ass!" He bled a bit. His dick was wet and nasty, but I sucked him anyway. He shot a load on my painter pants. He didn't want his wife to know. He asked me if I had a place. He wore black boxers with red Playboy bunnies on them. He wore a flannel shirt with the sleeves cut off. He said, "I'll cut your fucking throat." He was a fine piece of Mexican ass. He was such a cock tease. He wore a Silence=Death T-shirt. His wife seemed nice. He smelled like baby powder down there. He said, "Hold on to me while I come." He said to me, as I blew him, "I knew I would get some action tonight if I came here." He doesn't have the time for me now that his girlfriend has moved in. He likes to call me a *nigger* while I suck him off. He wants white, young dick only. His shaved balls. He has a black mouth for a white cock. He took a rubber out of the glove compartment. He was a hot, white male seeking same. He took his clothes off. His bare ass behind the bar. He stuck his dick under my stall. His wife wasn't home so my timing was perfect. He asked, "You didn't come in my ass did you?" He said that Jason Bartlett is a flaming faggot. (Whoever the hell Jason Bartlett is.) He drank too much. His name was Ronny. He loved to wear diapers and blue bonnets. He could fit a Ping-Pong ball up that ass. He put his shirt back on when I walked into the office. His big, Cuban dick. He videotaped us having sex. He was a virgin.

RIVERBOAT QUEENS

Dominic Santi

Most of the time, I'm straight. I mean, I love
my wife. I like fucking pussy. But there's something about being in LaCrosse that leaves
me starving for dick. On hot, muggy days in
July, I walk along the Mississippi and watch
the riverboats glide by. I hear the splash of
the paddle wheels and the cries of eagles flying past the sandstone cliffs. I feel the quiet
whoosh of barges moving slowly through the
thick, muddy water, and I remember my best
friend, Daryl.

Daryl and I grew up in the farm country east
of the river. Back at home, we were all just good
old boys. Sure, we knew about the straight/gay
things. We'd heard people call each other fag
or queer or gay on TV, even seen some guys
in dresses when we went to the Twin Cities on

our senior biology trip. The summer after we turned eighteen, though, Daryl and I were just buds hanging out together. We were single and horny and working hard out on his grandpa's farm, with no chicks around for miles and just a couple of well-thumbed *Playboy*s hidden out in the hayloft.

Back then, Daryl and I always jerked off together. It was just something we did.

"Fuck, look at the tits on this one. She is hot, dude. I bet she could suck the chrome off the shifter of your daddy's '68 T-bird." Daryl's breath wasn't exactly coming easy. He was lying back in the hay, naked except for his T-shirt and his socks. His short, stocky body glistened with sweat and strands of his long, sun-bleached hair clung to his neck. In one hand, he held the warped centerfold sideways, so Miss July five years ago hung down just above his cock. In the other, he held his thick, swollen shaft. As he spoke, he feverishly worked his foreskin back and forth over the glistening red tip beneath.

"Nice ass, too," I panted. My own dick was throbbing. I was taller and skinnier and darker than Daryl, so I figured it made sense that my dick was longer and thinner, with a thick nest of sweaty brown curls at the base. My cover wasn't long and loose like his either, but there was still enough there to get me shivering each time I pinched my skin and worked the web of frenulum beneath. I had a thing for tits, too. Even more than Daryl. My own especially. Daryl thought I was nuts. But when he saw how turned on I got, he'd chewed on my nipples more than once for me, so I'd have a really good come.

"Do me, man," he gasped, leaning back down into the stacked up hay. He tried to point the head of his dick toward me, but he was so hard it didn't want to go any direction but straight up. "I really need it, man. I am hard up for some serious cocksucking."

Now, Daryl and I had talked about this at length. When we'd heard some stuff on a special on TV, we'd been concerned we might turn gay if we kept sucking each other's dicks. Not that that bothered either one of us, really. But we were afraid that if we were gay, we wouldn't be able to fuck pussy anymore. And that would definitely not do. Not that either one of us had ever had a serious girlfriend, but it was the principle of the matter. So, after a lot of long and serious conversations over more than a few beers, we'd decided that sucking each other off was just a dick thing. It didn't have anything to do with liking either cocks or pussy. We were just horny. And as Daryl had said, I could see he was seriously hard up at the moment.

I tossed my magazine to the side and lay down on my shirt between his legs. As I took his balls in my hand and lifted them, Daryl threw his arm over his eyes. Now one thing I'll say about Daryl is that he really appreciated having his dick sucked. He moaned, long and sweet, as I licked into the damp heat between his ball sac and the side of his leg.

"Oh, dude," he groaned.

"You smell nice," I smiled, burying my face in his crotch and inhaling deeply. I licked long and slowly, swirling my tongue over the heavy orbs in his hot, wrinkled sac. "Taste good, too."

"Fuck," he moaned. Daryl wasn't real eloquent, at least not where his cock was concerned. As I started really working his balls, he reached down and stroked my hair. He buried his fingers deep, rubbing and tugging while I sucked his balls one at a time into my mouth and washed his salt from them with my spit.

We were never much into hurrying. As far as we were concerned, the first couple of hours after lunch were set aside for beating off. Nobody was going to venture into the barn to bother us during the heat of the day. So I sucked Daryl's nuts until he was moaning. The sweat on my shirt had dried, but I got it wet again with my precum as I wriggled over the thin cotton covering the thick hay beneath. Then I moved up just a bit and licked up his shaft.

"Oh, yeah, dude," he panted. "That's sweet."

And it was. Daryl's scent was one fucking intense aphrodisiac. The soft skin over his rock-hard dick was tangy and salty with his sweat and dried dick juices. We'd learned all about safer sex in school, but since neither one of us had ever had sex with anybody else, we figured we were safe. Besides, we didn't figure we were really having sex. We were just two guys beating off together and helping each other out. We especially didn't use the term *virgins*. No way. We had reps to uphold. And we would have slept with chicks, if there'd been any available, which there weren't. Well, except on Saturday nights. We both had reservations about the over-painted women twice our ages who came into town to party at the Barrel-On-Inn. And we definitely didn't want to go to church and get hitched, which was where the only chicks we knew who were our ages were. We figured things would get better when we went away to college in the fall. So, for now, we were just a couple of guys, helping each other out.

I licked up, teasing over the velvety soft skin, pointing my tongue down hard where the tube snaked up the middle of his shaft. With my thumb and forefinger, I pulled his dick-skin back. Then I flattened my tongue and licked on up into heaven.

"Oh, man!" Daryl was so sensitive, he jumped with each swipe. The thin layer of tangy sweat drew me like a cat to cream. He shook when I wiggled my tongue against the long, thin sensitive web underneath. "Do it softer, man. S-softer…"

I knew what Daryl needed. As I gentled my tongue, I let my saliva run down over his shaft. I drooled spit until his balls were wet and my mouth juice was running down into his crack. Daryl was breathing hard, panting like a dog. He knew what was coming. As I kissed my way tenderly up his shaft, he gripped my hair.

"Here it comes, dude." I opened my mouth and swallowed his cock. Daryl bucked up into my throat. Oh, god, he tasted good—salty and musky and something that was just plain him. His skin was soft and warm over the turgid flesh beneath. Each time I dove forward, his hips thrust up to meet me. I slid my finger down his straining balls and over the spit I'd drooled into his crack. Daryl didn't like to admit how sensitive his asshole was, so we didn't talk about it. But as soon as I started rubbing his perineum, his legs moved apart and he bent and lifted his knees. I rubbed the quivering, wrinkled pucker hiding between his asscheeks. He thrust deep into my throat, grunting as I swallowed him so deep I fought to keep from gagging.

Daryl never lasted long once I was fingering his hole. As my throat closed around him, I ground my throbbing cock into the sweaty shirt beneath me. I eased my slippery finger through that tight-assed sphincter of his and up into his wet, hot chute. Every damn time, he shouted, bucking up as his creamy jism spurted into my mouth. No matter how many times we did it, and we did it damn near every day, each time, I loved the feel of his semen squirting down my throat so much that right then and there, I came into that fucking shirt beneath my legs. There was a spot in Daryl's ass that made him squirt buckets when I massaged it, so while he writhed and twisted and my dick spurted into the crusty, well-used shirt, I rubbed that knot in his ass and sucked his cock while he held my head and fucked himself dry into my throat.

Then, no matter how many times I told him I'd already come, Daryl would announce that my coming into the shirt didn't count. Our helping each other was only fair if he got me off, too. He was shorter, but he was definitely stronger. So when he'd caught his breath and finally stopped shaking, he rolled me over and took my cum-covered cock in his mouth. He spit on his fingers until they were dripping. Then he worked them slowly and deliberately up my ass, one at a time until he had three or four in me, and he finger-fucked me while he sucked me off until I finally came again.

Even though I was young and horny, I'd just come, so sometimes it took me a really long time. Sometimes, it took so long Daryl would get hard all over again. So, when his fingers got tired, he spit on his dick and used that instead. It wasn't sex. It was just that his fingers were tired and he was horny again, too. So he grabbed my ankles and spread my legs, and he pressed his spit-covered dick into me. He pumped his big hard dick through my asslips and deep inside to press over that spot where my orgasms started. I grabbed my dick and squeezed it while he thrust hard and deep and fast, or sometimes slow and easy and relentlessly. When the orgasm finally boiled up out of me, my body stiffened and shook. My balls drained themselves dry while I grunted and twitched and tried not to yell because it felt so damn fucking good. Then Daryl stiffened over me and I felt the surges while he emptied himself up my ass.

We never talked afterward. That would have made what we were doing too much like sex. So we just lay there holding each other until we fell asleep. And when we woke up later on, we laughed at how sticky and sweaty our bodies were, and how the loft smelled like cum. Then we hid our *Playboys* and went back downstairs to work. And the next day, after lunch, we went back up to the loft and did it all over again.

For all I know, we might have been doing it still. But when fall came, Daryl and I went away to different colleges. He was killed by a drunk driver a few months later. During my sophomore year, I met Amy. We got married right after graduation and moved to Madison. She doesn't suck my cock as well as Daryl did, and I don't think she knows I have an asshole. But she has big breasts and a sweet pussy and I love her. Even though she never met Daryl, she didn't mind when I told her that I love her now, but I think I loved him that one summer so long ago, back when he and I were just eighteen.

And every summer, at least once, I find a reason to go to La-Crosse by myself to watch the riverboats moving up and down the Mississippi. I walk by the river on sultry afternoons and one way or another, I end up hooking up with another man. Now, I use condoms, even for sucking. I usually only come once. And I call what I'm doing sex. But when a warm, living dick is buried deep in my ass and I'm squeezing my dick, I think of Daryl. I hear the horns of the riverboats, and, oh, god, I come.

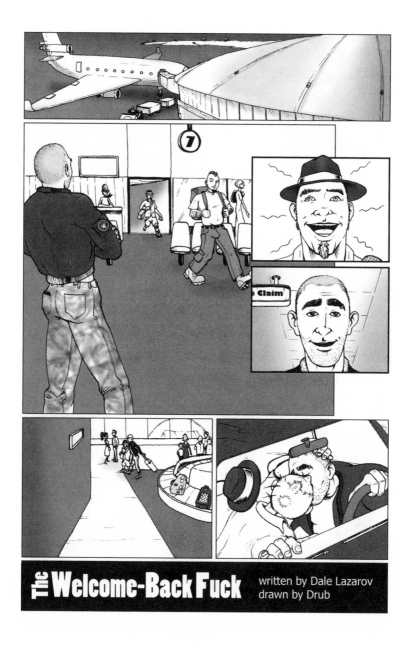

The Welcome-Back Fuck

written by Dale Lazarov
drawn by Drub

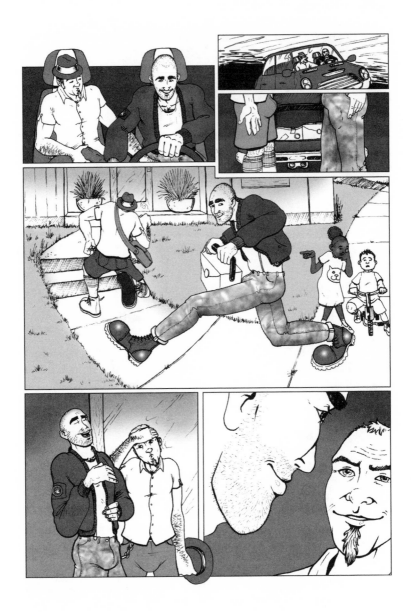

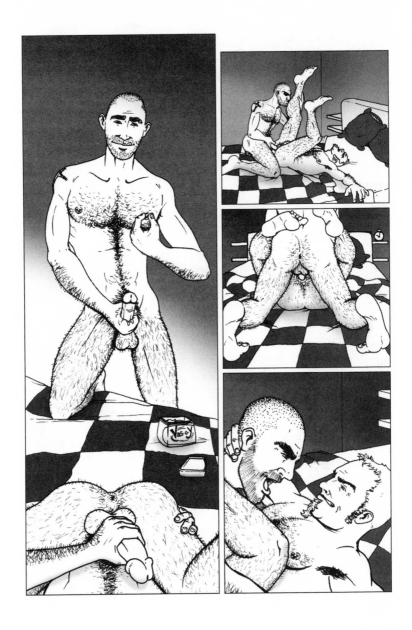

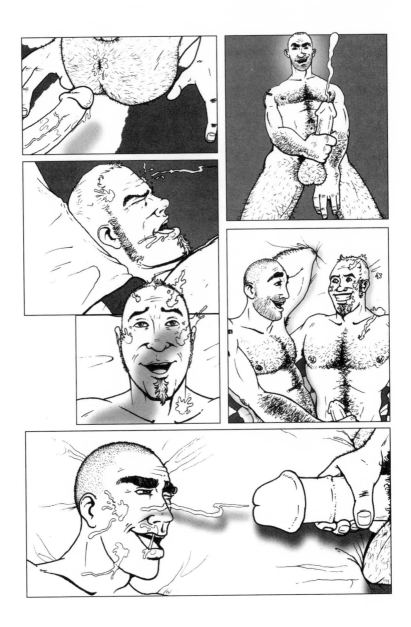

HOT SALES GUY

Alex Strand

Thursday, October 6, 2005: The Pillow Fight

Our business meeting went great. I'm certain we saved the client and we'll probably get more business out of them too. We had a slightly rocky start when someone mentioned politics and Bethany started to go on about "poor Mr. DeLay" and how he was being set up, "railroaded by partisan politics," she said, but Hot Sales Guy deftly cut her off and brought the meeting back on track. But I know that you could all give a shit about the business; you want to know what happened with Hot Sales Guy. Well, the best way to sum it up is that it was weird.

After dinner with the clients Bethany turned in to call her kids and pray or something and Hot Sales Guy and I decided to go out for a few drinks. We ran up to our rooms to change and and then meet back in the lobby. I put on my new Paper Denim & Cloth jeans, which, if I do say so myself, make my ass look awesome. Like Missy Elliott says, I feel like they make my "ass go boom!" I also wore the Rogues Gallery T-shirt that Hot Sales Guy got me for my birthday that says DEATH & CO. on the front—I love it. When we met up in the lobby it was about ten and after some hemming and hawing we decided we were too lazy to go out and we hit the hotel bar.

We had a pretty good time except when some fat asshole in a cowboy hat with a massive gut hanging over what I must say was a totally hip belt buckle (although I'm sure he didn't know that) drunkenly asked if us "girls" were having a good time. I ignored him but Hot Sales Guy turned toward him and said, "What?" in a confrontational way.

The guy laughed a little but then realized that Hot Sales Guy was serious. "Relax mister," he said nervously, "I just don't always see such pretty boys."

I was like, "Just ignore him. He's a drunk hillbilly."

Hot Sales Guy, his masculinity bruised, wanted to get into something but the guy was already looking the other way, no doubt dreaming up another stupid thing to say. So to take his mind off it I ordered tequila shots and pulled him into his seat.

At around eleven forty-five the bar was empty and the bartender told us it was last call. Hot Sales Guy and I were lit and wanted to keep going. He wanted to go into town and find a fun bar to do some "cruising," as he said. I was like, "Do you even know what 'cruising' is?"

"Sure I do. It's lookin' for chicks."

"Well, I guess," I said. "But mostly gay boys use it when we're looking to get laid."

"That's cool. I'm looking to get laid."

"By a gay guy?"

"Hold your horses there, big guy," was his response.

Trying to think quickly and strategically while drunk, which isn't easy, I managed to convince him that it was too much hassle to go out and find a bar and everything and that we should just go to one of our rooms and abuse the minibar. I told him my theory that we had done so well with the business that Bitch Boss wouldn't say anything about the bill. He said that was fine and we started upstairs. In the elevator I was like, "Whose room?" and he said, "Yours."

Inside we each kicked off our shoes and hit the bar. The assortment was pathetic, but there were three beers so that's where we started. I turned on the TV and we flipped through a bunch of stations and then clicked it off when we realized there was nothing to watch. I hooked up my little travel speakers to my iPod and we listened to some tunes instead. We talked about music, about Bethany, about Bitch Boss, and about how he thought one of the clients was hot. It was then—if you can believe it (straight guys are *so* slow)—that he noticed that I was wearing the T-shirt he'd given me. I of course was on the verge of mentioning it all night but I wanted him to notice. When he did I played it off like no big deal. "Oh yeah, it's a great shirt."

"Yeah," he said, his eyes a little droopy. "It looks good on you."

What? I was screaming inside. Nothing like a comment like *that* from *him* to knock some sobriety into me. I recalibrated myself and said as casually as I could, "You think?"

"Yeah," he said. "I mean don't let it go to your head or anything. I'd look better in it."

"As if," I said.

"Whatever, guy, you know I'd look tasty in it." And he smiled at himself and then downed the rest of his beer. That was already his second beer so there were no others left. He moved on to the twist-top wine.

"Dude," I said, "you're too old. You've got to be tight to pull this off." Of course I was full of shit; he'd look good in a car-cover, but it was tantalizing to tease him like that.

Still standing by the minibar with his twist-top wine, he was like, "I'm totally tight man, Don't give me that shit." And he pulled up the bottom of his shirt to show me his abs. He slapped them a few times and I wished it was my hand doing the slapping.

I rolled my eyes and raised an eyebrow like only a really good bitch can do and said, "Seen better."

"What're you talkin' 'bout? I've got it going on, dude. This bod brings in the ladies."

"Well that's good because you wouldn't last ten seconds in a gay bar. We're much more discerning."

"What? You ain't any better."

I rolled my eyes again, dismissing him, and drank up the rest of my beer. I walked into the bathroom to get a cup so that I could partake of the twist-top wine and I heard him holler after me, "I do one hundred crunches every fucking day." And when I walked back into the room he had his shirt up again and was punching his own stomach. "Rock solid," he said. "Rock solid."

"Whatever, dude. Keep your clothes on," I said, meaning exactly the opposite.

"Dude, you'd be lucky to get a piece of this."

"I get much better," I said. "Regularly."

"How many sit-ups you do every day?"

He just wouldn't let the stomach thing go; clearly I'd hit a nerve. "Enough, will you chill?"

He walked over to me and put his palm against my stomach, judging my firmness I suppose. I had a massive boner strapped down by my tight boxer-briefs. "Not so tight," he said.

"Is this a competition? Who's more butch?" I asked. I pulled my T-shirt off and said, "Let's see what you've got to offer." I tried to puff out my chest as best I could and flex my abs while he unbuttoned his shirt. My heart was beating a mile a minute. He dropped his shirt on the floor and started posing like the one of the guys on the WWE. I thought I was going to cum in my pants. Then he started grunting and making weird faces as he flexed. Straight men are so banal. "All right, chill out, Hulk Hogan."

"Dude, admit it, I'm pumped."

"You're drunk is what you are. But I guess I take it back: maybe there's a gay guy who'd do you."

"Maybe?"

"I'm sure there's some overweight pervert with braces and acne out there who'd let you take his ass for a spin."

He laughed and told me to fuck off. Then he took one of the pillows off the bed and hit me with it. I put up my hands to protect myself and then turned to the bed and dove for a pillow of my own. While I was on the bed I threw the first pillow at him and reached for another. He got on the bed on his knees, towering over me, and started pummeling me with his pillow. I was holding one up as defense while I kicked at him with my foot. I managed to knock him off balance and off the bed and I was able to get in a few good pillow-blows to his face. We were both panting, out of breath and laughing at the same time.

Then he charged me, wrapped his arms around me, and pushed me back onto the bed. He pinned me down so that he was on top, and started hitting me with the pillow. I was too busy thanking god for putting me in this position—with Hot Sales Guy straddling my crotch—to fight back; he managed to hold his pillow down over my face. I was totally leaking precum and my cock hurt trapped inside my boxer-briefs and jeans. I figured he had to feel my boner, his thigh was resting against it, but he didn't act like he noticed it. Trying to break free, I was grabbing at his back and arms, feeling their strength and muscular suppleness while sort of trying to pull him off me, but not really trying very hard.

Finally I got out from under his pillow, wrapped my arms around his abdominals and got him onto his side. I had my arm up on top of his side and I was leaning against him, holding him down, and trying to win the fight. I was momentarily transfixed by the view of his pecs and his nipple while his muscular arm was fighting me, and he somehow got out from underneath me and pinned me down again. I sort of surrendered, hoping he'd rape me or something; he got me facedown on the bed and twisted one arm behind my back. He made me call uncle before he'd let me go. Like I wanted him to let me go, please; I kept yelling "Aunt!" instead. Every time I did he pulled my arm tighter and tighter until finally I had to say uncle or risk seriously injuring my arm and shoulder. (I did think about risking the injury....)

He got off me and then off the bed. I turned over and watched as he walked back to the chaise lounge thing and slouched down into it. He didn't put his shirt back on, which was fine with me. "You're lucky I wasn't trying," I said, "or I'd have kicked your ass."

"Sure thing there, big guy," he said, grinning.

We were both out of breath and my cock was pulsing so hard I looked down at my pants for a wet spot. There was none—thank god. I went to the bar and opened the other twist-top bottle of wine. We turned the TV back on and he surfed the channels for a little while. I was staring at the TV, not really registering anything, just going over the pillow fight of my dreams in my head. Then I tried to turn my attention to getting the massive hard-on that was still throbbing in my jeans to subside.

I started focusing on the TV when a Bowflex commercial came on. They showed this ridiculously ripped guy using the machine and they were saying for just twenty minutes a day, three times a week, you could look like that. *Bull-fucking-shit,* I thought. That model probably spent half his fucking life at the gym and never ate anything other than raw fish and meat. I looked over at Hot Sales Guy to make some comment about the suckers that would believe that shit and he was totally passed out. His head was hanging back in what looked like a really uncomfortable position, and his mouth was wide open. I called his name but he didn't answer. I called it again louder, still no answer.

I got up and walked over to the chaise. He was wearing only his pants, belt, and socks, and he was absolutely beautiful. His chest was rising with each breath and I was close enough to see the tiny hairs on his beefy forearms. He started to snore a little and I jumped, feeling like I had been caught. But he was out. I poked his shoulder and called his name again and got no response. The snoring continued and then stopped and then started up again. I went back to the bed rubbing my hard-on through my jeans and flipped through the channels for a little while. I kept turning to look at him and he kept being passed out.

I watched an old episode of "The Golden Girls"—I know, *so* gay—and finished the wine. My cock was pulsing—it needed to shoot. I got up and went over to Hot Sales Guy and shook his shoulder and called his name again. No response. He was out like a light. I went back to my bed and my heart was pounding. I was really nervous. Should I do what I wanted to do?

I unzipped my pants, pulled down my boxer-briefs, and released my prick. It was hard and dripping and red from the excitement. I was leaning there against my bed, just a few feet away from him, and playing with myself. It was too much to handle: the visual of him and the feelings in my dick. I pulled up my jeans and put my cock away; I was so afraid of getting caught.

I walked back over to him and once again tried to shake him awake and got no response. So I just went for it. Like I was diving into an icy cold pool, I held my breath and unbuckled his belt. He didn't move. I unbuttoned his jeans and he still didn't move. I unzipped his jeans and almost had a heart attack I was so excited and scared of being caught at the same time. I pulled his pants open and saw that he was wearing regular boxers. Fuck it, I thought, I'd come this far. I pried open the fly of his boxers and got a good look at his sleepy, soft cock. I touched his stomach below his belly button and ran my hand along the top of his boxers. I then took my hand and moved it up to his brawny chest and cupped one of his pecs and lightly grazed the nipple with my thumb. This was too much, I kind of felt like I was violating him and I had to stop.

I pulled his boxers open as far as I could so that I could

see his cock resting there. Then I walked back to the bed and pulled out my cock. I spit in my hand and knew it would be like a five-second stroke off. While staring at the more than half-naked object of my obsession I had the hottest and shortest jack-off session of my life. I shot like a fucking geyser while staring at his hard body. I came onto the floor and all over my hand and my jeans and the nightstand. I couldn't stop cumming and right in the middle I imagined him waking up and seeing me and what he'd say. So fucking intense. After my orgasm was finally over, and I had a few aftershocks, I pulled up my jeans, wiped my hands on the bed, and went back over to him. I zipped his jeans and buttoned them again and buckled his belt. He still hadn't moved, he was still snoring, and I leaned over and kissed his lips lightly.

I put a blanket on him and went into the bathroom and got undressed. I was like, *Holy shit,* and I couldn't get my heart to calm down. I felt weird about the whole thing. Was I some pervert? Why had that been so fucking hot? Was there something wrong with me?

I went back out and got into bed. I tried to sleep but my mind was racing. Eventually I must have fallen asleep because I was awoken at about seven thirty by a groan. I looked over at the chaise and he was starting to sit up, his head in his hands. He looked up at me and raised his eyebrows in a "hey" gesture. I rolled over facing away from him and told him to go back to sleep; we still had a few hours before we had to get to the airport. He got up and I heard a whole bunch of rustling—he must have been putting on his shirt. He said he'd see me later and walked out the door

Oh my fucking god. The minute he was out the door I whipped out my cock and jerked off again.

Tuesday, November 29, 2005: Away with Hot Sales Guy

I just found out today that on Thursday Hot Sales Guy and I have to fly to Oklahoma City together for the night. I hadn't seen him since I'd been back and when he came into my office this afternoon, his hot fucking body bursting out of his clothes, my heart skipped a few beats and all the blood in my body rushed to my cock. Seemingly oblivious to his effect on me, he plopped himself down in a chair across from my desk and leaned back in one of those straight-guy leg-spreads. I could see the bulge of his cock all scrunched up and trapped in his pants and it was everything I could do not to jump over the desk and let that puppy free. But that was not to be. Instead we talked about our trip; or I should say, he talked about our trip and I stared at every inch of him. He told me that he had booked us rooms (and yes, unfortunately that word was plural) and flights and left the info with me. He told me we'd have fun, that we'd have a few drinks and unwind after we were done with the client. Then he left my office and I watched his ass until it was well out the door.

Needless to say I was a little preoccupied for the rest of the afternoon. All I could think about was the pillow fight and him nearly naked and how I had had the balls to jack off right next to his naked body. By the time I got home I had a raging boner that wouldn't subside. It almost felt like I was going to break my cock off as I walked. When I got inside I tried to put my mind to other things but it didn't work. I knew it wouldn't; I knew I'd have to take matters into my own hands.

So I went to my computer and booted up Jake Cruise. I had watched his new buff, hairy guy video Sunday night when I got home and was reminded of how great his site is. One of the best things about it is that you can save the videos you download and play them forever—even when you're not paying anymore. The two-load-worthy video I found tonight while cruising though his archives made it onto my hard drive for keeps. Anyway, Jason and Mikael were the boys I found and let me say: Yum.

Jason and Mikael had soloed for Cruise before but neither had ever done any real gay shit. This video was one of his gay-for-a-day or gay-for-pay movies and for enough cash he had gotten them to shoot an incredibly hot video. They blew each other and fucked and all the standard stuff that straight guys do to each other when they're bribed with a boatload of cash, but the hottest part was them making out. Two handsome straight guys making out is always an amazing sight. Throw in some fucking and sucking and, well, you've got a celebrity-chef-worthy recipe.

So the video was a little too hot and I blew my load after like ten minutes—but I didn't feel like I was done yet. I was still so horny and I felt like there was still a bunch of cum trapped in there that needed to get out; my boner didn't really subside. So what else was I going to do? I kept watching, got some more lube, and started stroking off again. By the end of the flick I was ready to pound out load number two. Wow.

But despite how hot the video was, I knew that Hot Sales Guy had a lot to do with those two loads. In fact, I had a feeling that when I climbed into bed, I'd be rubbing out load number three.

Thursday, May 18, 2006: Hot Sales Guy Makes Me Hard
God. I just want to lick him all over.

Hot Sales Guy and I spent about two hours this morning working on this presentation we have to do in a few weeks.

He just radiates sexiness and I can't keep my dick soft around him for more than five minutes. A few times while he was talking my mind wandered and I got fixated on his nipple pressing against his shirt or on the cords of his neck disappearing into his shirt. Then I'd realize he'd been quiet for a minute and was waiting for me to respond, and like in a sitcom I'd have no clue what he'd said. Eventually we'd get back on track and then I'd have to spend the next ten minutes thinking about dead bunnies and mass travel accidents, trying to get my boner to subside.

We took a break around noon and went to lunch. I was staring at his beautiful body, so tightly wrapped in much less beautiful clothes, and I was marveling over his diet. He had a double cheeseburger with bacon and fries. I meekly ate my grilled chicken salad with balsamic vinegar and thought how unfair it was that he can eat anything and look like he does while I have to eat roughage and vinegar with a fancy name to stay trim. I was thinking that I should start a diet of my own. Kind of like the Atkins diet but I'd call it the Alex diet and it would be an all-cock diet. I had it all figured out: you'd save your bigger cocks for lunchtime when you are supposed to eat your largest meal, therefore giving yourself time to metabolize it properly. Then, for dinner and breakfast, you'd try to stick to some smaller cocks for lighter meals. And to be certain that your diet was balanced you would make sure to incorporate cocks from multiple food groups, such as: black, hispanic, caucasian, and asian. For snack time you could munch on a nipple or take a lick at some nonfat abs and then if you were really good you could munch on some warm ass for dessert.

Do you ever wonder how the shit that goes through your head gets there? I mean, how random was this dumb diet I was thinking about? I must have smiled or something and Hot Sales Guy was like, "What?"

Feeling like a total lunatic, and not wanting him to think I was a cannibal or something, I told him I was thinking about a guy I fucked around with last night.

"Tiny cock?" he asked.

"Huh?"

"Is that what's funny? Didn't measure up?"

"No—"

He cut me off before I could say more and puffed his chest out and said in a half-joking, half-not manner, "Not everyone can be hung like me."

"Please..." I said, remembering the tent in his shorts I'd been lucky enough to see a few times. "Spare me."

"Then what was his problem?"

I told him the story about how the guy was a little weird and standoffish and afraid to be naked, but that I still found him and the whole scene hot. Despite the conservative slant, he still did it for me, I told him.

"Jesus...who doesn't do it for you?" he asked.

Lying like the biggest motherfucker ever—Pinocchio's nose would've wrapped around the earth twenty times from a lie this big—I said, "You."

He laughed and said, "Yeah right. Like you're not jonesing for a crack at me."

"If you're lucky, stud, I'll lower my standards one of these days."

"You'd be the lucky one and you know it," he said.

Back at the office I couldn't stop thinking about him and our lunch and our conversation. I totally read too much into things but I mean he was totally flirting, right? What straight guy says shit like that to his gay friend? Especially when he knows that there is something weird there?

Anyway, when I got back from lunch I had this thumping, distracting boner I had to do something about. I walked into my office and closed and locked my door. I leaned up against the closed door and undid my belt and then my pants. I let my pants drop around my ankles and I pushed down my underwear and I leaned my naked ass against the door. I spit in my hand and wrapped it around my cock and started to stroke. I couldn't do it slowly and I couldn't use much restraint.

I closed my eyes and thought of Hot Sales Guy sitting there at lunch and telling me how much he knows I want him. I imagined him getting up and unbuttoning his shirt and asking me if this is what I wanted; was his body what I wanted. I kept telling him yes. My hand was flying all over my cock and my other hand was yanking on my balls. I imagined him with his shirt off and his pants open now like in the hotel that night. I imagined him pulling them down slowly and releasing a giant boner that he would point at me and say, "Today's your lucky day."

I squeezed the base of my cock and then started to tickle my nuts as I imagined myself on my knees with him feeding me that hot cock. I was looking up at his stacked slabs of muscle and into his face that was lost in pleasure. I couldn't go much longer. I was holding my breath and jerking my dick in these really short intense strokes and then I came. I bit down on my tongue and I squeezed my cock as hard as I could and then I shot my load out onto the office floor.

I had gotten a little sweaty during my workout and my ass stuck to the door as I pulled myself away. I licked my cum off my hand and looked down at the mess on the floor. I pulled my pants up and buckled my belt and went to my desk for a paper towel. I was on my knees wiping up the mess when someone knocked on my door. I got totally nervous but I stood up and opened it. It was a lady named Judy who worked for me and she looked at me while I was holding the paper towel covered in cum. I asked her what she needed and made some excuse about the people who water the plants getting crap on the floor. I tossed the paper towel and got her what she needed. She didn't seem too suspicious even though she—hopefully unwittingly—stepped over some small dark stains on the carpet as she left.

I felt a little more relieved by the time Hot Sales Guy stopped by at four thirty to say good night. But then, watching his ass as he walked out of my office, I got rock hard again. Fuck…

THE LIGHTHOUSE KEEP:
A GOTHIC TALE

Jay Neal

At that time of year on the rocky coast of
Maine—not long after the summer solstice—
twilight extends well into the late evening.
However, it was now pushing on toward later
evening and a thick blanket of clouds, which
had already been responsible for several days
of rain in the area, conspired to make it a
dark and rather stormy night, as required by
the conventions of gothic literature.

Additional needed elements were in place
as well: the intrepid and unsuspecting traveler—yours truly—his transport in difficulty
—car stuck in mud at the side of the road—
trudging along in search of assistance. Sure
enough, I finally spotted a light glowing in the
window of a not-too-distant cottage.

A cottage, mind you, situated next to a

dark, looming lighthouse that obviously hadn't operated in years. I dragged myself toward the cottage, the sound of surf crashing against rocks growing louder with each step.

I knocked loudly at the door of the cottage, which precipitated some loud crashing noises and considerable swearing within. At last the door creaked open and I was facing a short, gnarly man of indeterminate age. His face was a fine collection of wrinkles on weathered skin, largely obscured by a silvery beard that descended halfway down his chest. However, he couldn't have been more than an inch over five feet tall. The gnomish effect was completed by a knitted cap pulled over a mass of unruly silvery hair, and a pipe clenched in his teeth. To be honest, it was all I could do to keep from giggling.

"Arr," he said, "which it'll be: lost or car trouble?"

Arr? I thought. Was he for real? "Car trouble, actually. Stuck in the mud about half a mile back."

"Lot o' rain last few days. Makes lots o' mud. Best come in for the night. We can pull your car out come mornin'."

He opened the door wide to let me in then closed it quickly against the wind, which was beginning to howl around the corners of the cottage. Most of the small house was dark, so he led me into the kitchen and invited me to sit at the table.

"Coffee?" he offered.

"Yes, that sounds wonderful."

He poured some dark, thick liquid into an enameled mug and set it in front of me.

"Looks like we're in for a storm tonight," he said as he sat at the table.

"Red sky at night, sailor's delight...?"

He cocked his head at me for a moment before answering.

"Er, no, I saw it on the Weather Channel." He tried not to look smug; I felt suitably chastened.

"Do you keep the lighthouse?" I ventured.

"Arr, no, I broker real estate in Connecticut, Massachusetts, and New Hampshire. The Internet has been very liberating for me, let's me telecommute."

So far the score was intrepid traveler: 0, gnarly old man: 2.

"But," I protested, "that was an old lighthouse I saw outside, wasn't it?"

"Arr, that it were, that it were. And," he puffed on his pipe and then took it out of his mouth to point the stem at me, "therein lies a tale you'll be wantin' to hear."

Oh good, here it came. "Yes, of course." I picked up my mug of coffee, using it to warm both my hands.

He began: "It's a tale of unnatural love and tragedy that was the biggest scandal around these parts for years before or after." He was evidently well practiced at telling his story, and clearly relished the chance to tell it again.

"This lighthouse last shone its light on a warm summer evening in July 1889, the night of the new moon and doubly treacherous for sailors.

"The retired Captain of a whaling fleet lived then in this house. He had been successful at his work, retiring in his early forties. When he was on land he preferred the seclusion of these modest and remote surroundings.

"Living in a room over in the lighthouse was the lighthouse Keep, by all accounts a big, rugged bear of a man with fiery red hair. Many's the time the Keep and the Captain would share meals and companionable times together, despite the differences in their social backgrounds. No one knew it at the time, but it all came out afterward that the Captain and the

Keep were secretly lovers, and had been for nearly eighteen years by that summer.

"Earlier that spring, a young nephew of the Captain, barely sixteen years old, came to live as a Ward of the Captain. He had recently been orphaned when his parents were killed in a tragic accident. The Ward took to these remote surroundings and quickly recovered his youthful zest for life. The three of them seemed to find comfort and delight in each other's company.

"But their idyllic arrangement was not to last. As the summer unfolded, it seems that the Keep developed an unquenchable carnal lust for the Ward. The Keep had also begun to harbor peculiar notions about how to rejuvenate his own body to regain his youthful vigor, notions that involved mystical, sadistic rituals, according to some. These two unstoppable forces in the Keep's mind finally collided on the night of that new moon in July.

"The Captain, you see, had been called away to consult with the government, for whom he served as an adviser on nautical matters. He was gone for several days, returning two days earlier than expected.

"He arrived late, well after dark, but was surprised to find his house dark and—verified by a brief search—deserted. Perhaps his Ward and the Keep were in the lighthouse, swapping late-night stories and playing cards, as they often had before. Sure enough, he saw candlelight flickering through the open door of the lighthouse as he walked toward it.

"However, the sight that greeted his eyes when he reached the door was far from the innocent recreation he had imagined. He saw his Ward manacled to some infernal machine, totally naked, with numerous welts visible on his flesh; the lad may even have been unconscious by that time.

"The Keep, himself totally naked save for leather boots and a leather mask, held a bullwhip in his hand, intent on his deviant ritual.

"Outraged, the Captain cried out for a halt to the diabolical proceedings. Startled by the intrusion, the Keep dropped his whip and ran up the stairs toward the top of the lighthouse.

"Now in a fit of jealous rage at the Keep's betrayal, the Captain pursued the Keep to the top of the lighthouse. What really happened there, we'll never know. The official story was that the Keep, faced with the certain revelation of his proclivities, jumped to his death on the rocks far below. Unofficially, most folks around here believe that the Captain threw the Keep over the railing himself, but none could fault him for it.

"That night, the lighthouse went dark and was never illuminated again. The Captain nursed his Ward back to health. The Ward never spoke of the incident, nor gave any indication that he even remembered any of the events of that night. The Captain never regained his former spirit; he died just a few years later, a diminished and broken man. The Ward eventually got married and continued to live in this house—he was my great-grandfather. And legend has it that, on nights of the new moon, the ghost of the Keep prowls restlessly about the lighthouse, hoping to consummate his bizarre ritual."

He finished his tale and puffed on his pipe with satisfaction, waiting for my predictable response.

"Shocking!" I said, shaking my head.

He nodded. "Arr, that it were, that it were."

"I don't suppose," I ventured, "that tonight, by any chance, happens to be a new moon?"

Again he nodded. "Arr, that it is." Suddenly he whipped the pipe from his mouth and leaned across the table, a look of earnest urgency on his face. "You might wish to mock my tale, but you would be wise not to go near the lighthouse tonight."

I was a bit taken aback. "I certainly won't."

"Good, good. Well, let's get you into bed, safely tucked away from this old man's ghost stories. We'll have an early morning."

He pushed himself up wearily from the table and led me to a small room off the kitchen. It was furnished with a small table and chair and a single bed already made up.

"Heed my warning and have a good sleep," he said as he withdrew from the room, closing the door behind him.

I was, indeed, terribly fatigued, so I got out of my clothes quickly, slipped into bed, and turned off the bedside lamp. The bed was surprisingly comfortable, and the blankets warm and cozy. I barely had time to hear the old man climb the stairs to this own room before I fell into a deep sleep.

I don't know what brought me so quickly out of my deep slumber, but I awoke to the sound of a loose window shutter banging against the cottage. Apparently the storm was underway and it was windy. I got out of bed and pulled on my trousers to investigate.

I looked in vain through the kitchen windows for a loose shutter, but by then the banging had stopped anyway. However, my attention was drawn toward the lighthouse, where a warm glow spilled from an open door, a light such as might have come from a multitude of candles.

As I watched I was startled to see a shadow come and go,

as though someone were pacing just inside the lighthouse door. Without much thought, I imagined that my host was preparing a display to enhance his ghost story.

Woooooo! *Heed my warning and do not approach the lighthouse* indeed. *Booga! Booga!* I thought in response. Then I did exactly what I shouldn't have: I disregarded my host's stern warning, went out the kitchen door, and walked toward the lighthouse. As I drew closer, I had the fanciful notion that the light from the door had mystical, magnetic powers pulling me inexorably closer. Perhaps such notions were the result of strong coffee and gothic tales before bedtime.

I reached the lighthouse and stood in wonder outside the doorway. What I had expected was nothing to do with the reality that confronted me. Directly opposite the door, built into the curve of the staircase that spiraled along the outside wall, was a large wooden device built of substantial timbers, each some six or seven feet long, in the shape of a large X. The extremity of each timber was wrapped with chains, attached to which there appeared to be leather straps.

In front of the wooden device, in the center of the floor, lay an enormous bullwhip, resembling nothing so much as a very large, very scary snake lying in wait for prey. Spooky and intimidating.

As I had imagined, the entire scene was illuminated by what must have been a hundred candles. There were candles everywhere, in candlesticks, on steps, hanging from sconces, and simply sitting on the floor. As before, I felt mysteriously drawn by the light to step through the door.

I had read enough of these types of stories to know what was about to happen, but I guess I thought surely not this time, not here. This is reality, after all, not gothic fiction.

Suddenly the light went out—an opaque bag had been thrown over my head. I couldn't remove it, because now someone much stronger than I was holding my arms pinned behind me. The last thing I remember is something like a smell of mint, and then I blacked out.

As consciousness returned, I felt groggy and sluggish and in no hurry to wake up. For some reason, my shoulders ached. I had just turned my head and cracked an eyelid to see why when I heard the crack of a whip and felt something tickle my left nipple.

Awareness returned in a flood and my eyes popped open. I barely had time to register the presence standing before me, nor realize the consequence of his drawing back the hand holding the whip, before there was another crack and a sensation at my left nipple like a fluttering tongue.

Despite his obvious skill with the whip, I wasn't convinced that this game's odds were in my favor. Sooner or later this whip business was likely to prove painful, and I don't do pain very well.

The whole situation was wholly unreal. Could I have predicted a week ago that tonight I would find myself in an abandoned lighthouse, stripped naked—had I mentioned that?—lashed to a St. Andrew's cross, experiencing foreplay-at-a-distance through the agency of an eight-foot bullwhip?

He pulled back his whip hand and—crack!—I felt a touch light as a feather across my balls. Hey! This was getting serious!

Who was this guy anyway? I'd vaguely been thinking it would be my host, but this clearly was not the gnarly old man. No, this apparition was well over six feet tall, with shoulders nearly as broad as the lighthouse door and a burly build to match. His body was covered with flaming red hair, at least all the parts that I could see, which was most of him since the sum total of what he wore was: leather gloves, knee-high leather boots, and a leather hood that covered the top half of his head but stopped short of the full, red beard that covered the rest of his face.

Certainly he could be described as a "big bear of a man." Was this meant to be the prowling ghost of the lighthouse Keep here to consummate his eternally frustrated ritual?

Once again he primed his whip, once again with the ear-splitting crack, and I felt a gentle tweak at the tip of my dick. My first reaction was to complain that this dangerous farce had gone on long enough, but I was betrayed by my dick, which had grown full and very firm, in evident affirmation of this unique stimulation. Judging from the state of the Keep's own intimidating erection, it seemed to be working for him, too.

This foreplay with the whip seemed to be over. The Keep slowly, deliberately coiled it in his hand then stepped toward me. I was entranced by the sight of his heavy, meaty dick bobbing its head at each step.

He stepped right up until the tip of his hard-on touched the tip of mine. The feeling was electrifying. I stared into his eyes as he stared back into mine. I felt his warm breath fall down my chest and wondered: do ghosts breathe?

With the whip he gently caressed my dick, slow strokes up and down the entire shaft. At one point a drop of hot wax dropped onto my shoulder from a candle in the sconce hanging above my head. My dick jumped in surprise; the Keep snorted at my reaction.

Without warning he swiftly lifted his whip and coiled it two, perhaps three times around my throat. I was concerned about his intentions, but strangely aroused as well. My dick could not have been more engorged than it was right then.

He pulled just enough on the ends of the whip to tighten it slightly around my neck. At the same time he squatted somewhat and began working on my nipples. At first he merely licked and brushed them with his beard. Before long he began biting them, starting with light nibbles that got progressively firmer and, I might add, more painful and more pleasurable. Between my nipples and the whip wrapped around my throat, I was starting to feel light-headed. I was startled again when another drop of hot wax fell on my shoulder.

With another tug on the leather noose the Keep moved his attention to my very attentive erection. He sucked and licked, again with great deliberation, for many minutes while I concentrated on trying to breathe in enough air, a challenge I feared I was slowly losing.

Just as I felt certain to pass out—whether from lack of oxygen or in ecstasy or both—the Keep released his hold on the whip and pulled it free of my neck.

He dropped to the floor and positioned himself on his back with his head beneath my dick, his naked body stretched out on the floor in front of me. It was a sight I was sure to remember, provided I survived the night.

Again, he found a creative use for his whip. He grabbed the business end and coiled it a few times around my dick. When he held the two free ends and twisted them, the coil around my dick tightened into a leather sleeve that he used to jerk me off. At the same time he started stroking his own dick with the identical rhythm.

As I watched him jerk himself, it almost felt like his dick was an extension of my own, his perfect tempo taking me ever closer, ever so slowly, toward my own climax.

I was nearly there, and the Keep knew it. At the last moment, he released his hold on the coil around my dick, grabbed the butt end of the whip and pressed it against my asshole. I took a deep breath and tried to relax. With his insistent pressure the end of the whip slipped inside of me.

Suddenly, all my senses were overwhelmed. The room, the candles, the hot wax, my bondage, the vision of the Keep lying naked before me, the sight of him jerking his dick, the whip deep inside me—it was too much. He fucked me with only a few strokes of the whip before I came with a vengeance. Hot cum spewed from my dick, covering the Keep's prone body from his neck to his belly. Several more times he plunged in the whip, and each time I pumped out another load.

Here, then, was the consummation of his ritual, the elixir for which he eternally searched. He jerked himself off with maniacal fervor and in moments covered himself with his own copious amount of cum, pools of pearl-white liquid that merged with my own contributions.

We were exhausted, fully spent—at least, I was. I tried to relax, to slow my heartbeat, to regain normal breathing, to get the feeling back in my shoulders, and to see whether I might persuade the bullwhip, which still dangled from my butt, to slip out of my asshole.

Suddenly a gust of wind howled around the lighthouse, throwing shut the door then flinging it open again. The candles flickered ominously. The howl of the wind increased to a roar that sounded uncannily like an angry voice.

The reaction of the Keep was remarkable. As if in fear of the sound, he leapt to his feet and ran full out up the stairs toward the top of the lighthouse. I listened with increasing despair as the sound of his boots on the steps grew more distant and then vanished.

Five seconds, maybe ten, passed in silence and then another gust of wind howled around the lighthouse. This time, however, it created an unearthly and chilling sound disturbingly like a human scream. Was this the ghost of the Keep, falling once again to his death on the rocks below? Was he fated to endure the horror of his death for all eternity?

The sound of the scream receded. Suddenly, the silence was absolute, and I felt very alone, very abandoned. I had barely begun to worry about my predicament, when I noticed once again a faint odor of mint and passed out.

I awoke to find myself lying comfortably in my bed in the cottage, with bright morning sun streaming through the window. I heard someone, presumably the gnarly old man, moving about in the kitchen. He must have been preparing breakfast: there were sizzling sounds and the most welcome smell of bacon cooking. I quickly got up and threw on my clothes, noting that my arms were rather stiff around the shoulders.

I walked into the kitchen, relieved to see that it was the gnarly old man and not another apparition. He gestured for me to sit at the table, where he fed me a hearty meal of fried eggs and bacon. I ate with an unusually aggressive appetite.

Our conversation was minimal. At one point he looked in my eyes and pointedly asked, "So, I hope ye slept well and sound."

"Oh yes," I said with great conviction, "quite well indeed.

It must be the sea air."

He regarded me skeptically, but decided to pass on the cross-examination. "Arr, that it be, that it be."

We finished our meal in silence and drank the last of the coffee. Then he slapped the table and announced, "Well then, let's get the old truck fired up and go get you pulled out of the ditch."

"Sounds good to me."

KURT

Jonathan Asche

Thursday

I'm standing at my apartment door, trying to keep my hand steady as I put my key in the lock, when my new neighbor steps out. He looks at me as he locks his door, smiles and says hello. He's cute—I noticed that when I saw him moving in a couple of weeks ago—and, according to my gaydar and the rainbow sticker on the back window of his car, family.

I say hello back as I push my key in. He introduces himself, says his name is Jake and offers his hand. I transfer the bag I'm holding to my other hand and we shake. I offer a hasty *I'm-James-nice-to-meet-you*. I notice his interested smile, but he's too late. Had he introduced himself to me a week ago, I might've been more accommodating—giddy, even.

When he starts with the small talk I quickly excuse myself, saying I have some work I need to get caught up on, and open my apartment door.

"Okay," Jake says. "Maybe we could go out for coffee sometime?"

"Sure, yeah," I say, and close the door.

Minutes later, Kurt joins me. "I got here just in time," he says, stepping into my bedroom. I'm already naked, lying on the bed. I've got a porno DVD playing, the sound down low. "Looks like you were about to start without me."

"Just getting in the mood," I say, grabbing him. He's already hard. "Feels like you're in the mood already."

"I'm *always* in the mood."

I take Kurt's cock out, and even though this isn't the first time I've seen it, I'm awed by its size. I use both hands to map its length and girth, squeezing it gently, feeling the resistance of the turgid flesh. Then I bring my mouth to it, my tongue circling the plump crown. Opening wider, I take the dick inside. I want to deep-throat him, but he's so huge that I can only swallow five inches before I start gagging. I'm embarrassed by my failure, but Kurt's understanding, saying I don't have to take the whole thing at first, what I'm doing feels just fine.

So I suck the first five inches of Kurt's cock. I grab his balls, squeezing them cautiously at first, then harder at his urging; he tells me that a little pain makes the pleasure that much sweeter.

Kurt grabs my dick, and I must admit I'm embarrassed again. I'm average sized, but compared to him I might as well have a cocktail wienie. But Kurt makes me forget my inadequacies when he fondles my cock, my body trembling at the touch of his experienced fingers. He smears my precum around my pulsing cockhead, and then brings his fingers to my mouth; I taste my own juices. He pulls his fingers from my mouth and slips them between my spread thighs, sliding into my asscrack until he finds my hole. His wet fingers glaze my butthole, pushing against the muscled ring. When one of his fingers works its way inside, I whimper. Slowly, he slides the finger in and out, and my whimpers become moans.

He pulls his finger out of my ass and brings it to my mouth, saying I need to lube it up some more. So I suck the finger he was fucking me with, as well as the other four, until his hand is dripping with my spit. When that hand returns to my ass, two fingers go into my hole. As he finger-fucks me Kurt rubs his horsecock against my prick, asking me if I want more. I say yes, yes, begging.

I cover Kurt's pole with lube, stroking him playfully until he tells me to stop, saying I'll get him off too soon. I lie back on the bed and bring my legs up. First, Kurt rubs his lube-slick dong against the groove of my split ass, making my asshole pucker—and my cock drool—with anticipation. Anticipation becomes apprehension when he presses the head of that monster against my asslips. Taking a huge cock up your ass sounds hot in theory; the real thing trying to force its way in gives you second thoughts. I knew it would be difficult, but getting fucked by Kurt was more than worth the pain.

He applies pressure, forcing my asslips to open. I gnash my teeth as he pushes his way into me, crying out when his cockhead punches its way into my hole. My cock goes limp. Kurt waits a moment, letting me get used to him, letting that first shock of pain die down before he goes any further.

It's easier from there, Kurt sliding into me an inch at a time, my butt warming to the idea. He pushes on, my ass proving more accommodating than my throat: I take every last inch of him, right down to the base. His balls press against my ass.

My dick springs back to life, signaling to Kurt that all is okay. He starts pumping and I start writhing. My arousal ratchets upward each time he rams into me, leaving me breathless and gasping. I say things like, "Fuck me with that huge cock," knowing it's a stupid porno video line, but in the heat of the moment it doesn't sound so dumb.

Kurt rams into me harder and harder. He curls a hand around my aching prick, making my body shudder. He strokes my cock while he plows into my ass, the simultaneous sensations taking me so close to the brink it's impossible to fight it. My body jerks and I exhale a strained groan as I spew my hot load onto my belly. Kurt pushes into me with one decisive thrust, grunting. I squeeze my butt muscles against his shaft, holding him inside as he cums.

I close my eyes, drifting off to sleep, with Kurt's cock still buried inside me. I hear the performers in the porn DVD moaning and groaning and I smile, happy that I have the real thing.

The Following Saturday

The bell rings twice before I open the door. Jake is standing there, smiling. He's wearing a gray T-shirt with the logo of a popular gym chain emblazoned across the front, and judging by the way his chest pushes against the shirt's fabric, he's a regular patron.

"Hey there," he says, real friendly. "I was having a little get-together tonight—not really a party, just a few friends—and wanted to know if you'd like to come?"

"Well…"

"I'm having a Pia Zadora film festival," Jake giggles. "My friend Kyle just got a bootleg copy of *Voyage of the Rock*

Aliens, and of course I'm going to show *The Lonely Lady*. Christ, I've practically worn that tape out, but it's just so damn funny. And after a couple of margaritas and a toke or two, it's *hysterical*. So, will you join us? Please say yes."

There was a time when I wouldn't have to think twice about accepting such an invitation, especially from someone like Jake. A month ago, he could've asked me to go to church and I'd have run out and bought a Bible. I should be excited. Instead, I'm annoyed.

"I'd like to," I say, "but I've already made other plans."

"Oh. Okay." He doesn't try to hide his disappointment. "Some other time, then?"

"Sure," I say, closing the door.

Kurt's waiting for me in the bedroom. "Sorry for the interruption," I say, pulling off my shirt. "Every time I turn around, the phone's ringing, someone's at the door. Why can't I just be left alone?"

"You used to hate being alone," Kurt says.

"That was *alone* alone. But I love being alone with you." I pull off my shorts. "Now, where were we? That's right, on the floor."

I straddle a long, narrow mirror that I took down earlier from the closet door. My naked body looks back at me. I watch as Kurt positions himself behind me, his cock already hard—it's *always* hard—and lubed, the head nudging my asslips. That's all it takes for my cock to snap to, and I'm fascinated watching it swell, as if that's not me reflected in the mirror, but some third person joining us, a stranger with my identical body.

Kurt pushes his rod against my rosebud, my sphincter loosening. My ass is a lot less resistant, what with Kurt fucking me almost every day, sometimes twice. The cockhead pries open my hole, and his prick tunnels its way inside. I raise my ass and push backward, urging him in deeper. "That's it, baby, that's it," I pant. "All the way inside." I watch in the mirror as my butt swallows up his cock, watch as my own dick quivers, a thin, viscous thread of precum swinging from my piss slit.

I reach between my legs, grabbing Kurt's balls, pulling on them roughly so they touch my own swollen 'nads. My hips roll, up and down, while Kurt moves in and out. The pleasure is fiery and intense, making my legs weak. When Kurt grabs my cock, I almost collapse.

"I don't...I don't know how much longer I can last," I hiss, fighting the ticklish hint of an orgasm.

Kurt says nothing, just keeps fucking my ass and pulling on my dick.

"I'm going to cum," I warn.

He fucks me harder and strokes me faster.

I cry out and almost fall face-first onto the glass. Milky white drops rain down onto the mirror.

Kurt's dick pulses inside my chute. My eyes focus on different parts of the reflection beneath me: my ass-ring gripping the base of Kurt's rod; my cock, the crown capped with one stubborn drop of jizz; the puddles of cream cooling on the mirror's surface.

A command is issued, barely audible, and I have to listen for Kurt to repeat it. "Lick it up," he says.

I don't question and I don't protest. I move back, Kurt moving with me, until the face staring back at me is distorted by thick gobs of cum. Kurt, his cock still stuffed up my ass, leans to one side so he can watch as I lower my face to the mirror. My tongue touches down in one of the pools of spooge, and I lap it up in long, lusty licks, like a dog. Kurt pushes the back of my head until my nose is crushed against the mirror. I turn my head, my cheek sliding against the sticky-slick surface, and close my eyes. Kurt pumps my ass a few more times until he's done.

"That was awesome," he whispers.

I squeeze my ass against Kurt's swollen shaft, wanting to milk out every last drop of him. "You bring out the best in me," I sigh.

A Month Later

We pass Jake on the stairs; he's climbing up as we're heading down to the lobby. He's sorting through his mail, but looks up long enough to give me a quick hello and a tight smile. There are no invitations for a drink or to watch bad movies.

"That's the neighbor?" Kurt asks when Jake's out of ear-shot. "He's *hot.*"

"He's been kind of cold lately," I say.

"Why didn't you introduce us?"

"I want you all to myself."

"Selfish bitch," Kurt chuckles.

It's raining as we step outside the apartment building. I've forgotten my umbrella, but I don't go back for it. It's only a light drizzle, I reason, as Kurt and I start up the street in a trot, giggling like two schoolboys playing hooky. It's a testament to our relationship that I'm so happy these days. Given the circumstances, I should be morbidly depressed. I got fired last week for chronic absenteeism. I'd been calling in sick a lot so I could stay home and fool around with Kurt. I mean, who wouldn't? One week I didn't even call in, and that was the last straw, apparently. I've never been fired before, and have always been terrified by the prospect. But when I was handed a box containing the personal items from my desk and escorted out of the office, I actually smiled. Not having a job just gives me that much more time to spend with Kurt.

We're fairly well soaked by the time we reach our destination, Video XXXtra, where Kurt and I first met. Inside, it's bright and smells of plastic. We head right for the section with all the gay videos. Even though I have a specific title in mind, I wander the aisles, browsing. Shopping for porn is like picking someone up at a bar: no matter what you bring home, you always suspect you could've done better.

But Kurt's impatient. "Just get the one you talked about," he says. "You know it's hot."

Ultimately, that's what I do, taking the case up front and telling the unsmiling middle-aged woman behind the counter I want to use a viewing booth. She takes the DVD case and my money, telling me to go to booth number four.

"You don't think anyone saw you come in here with me, do you?" I whisper to Kurt when we're inside the booth. It's cramped, the smell of bleach almost masking the funky odor of stale spunk.

"I was careful," Kurt assures me. "And no one's going to see me cum *with* you in here, either."

Hearing Kurt say that makes my cock throb. I was getting hard as I was walking into the back room where the viewing booths are, and now I'm rigid. In the dark I reach for Kurt. His dick's out and hard as usual. "You're incredible," I whisper, stroking his shaft, bumpy with turgid veins.

The screen in front of me flickers to life, and a minute later I have my pants undone and my cock out. Kurt rubs his thick pole against my hard-on. "Ever been fucked in one of these things?" he asks.

"You *know* the answer to that," I whisper. "I've never been in one of these things, period. They always seemed spooky. I wouldn't be in one now if you hadn't suggested it."

I sit down on the booth's vinyl-covered bench. Kurt, kneeling between my legs, undulates against my body, the weight of his cock rubbing against my own engorged prick, creating a heated friction. "Don't look now, but we've got a visitor," he says.

A glance to my right and I see what he's talking about. The guy in the neighboring booth has stuck his cock through the glory hole in the wall, beckoning my attention. I'm at once mortified and intrigued.

"Suck it," Kurt encourages.

"But..."

"I think it would be hot, you sucking some stranger's cock while I fuck you from behind. C'mon, don't pretend you don't want to."

He's right. Kurt knows me so well. I turn and kneel on the floor. Kurt pushes my pants down, and while he fingers my hole with two spit-lubed fingers, I regard the stiff pole in front of me. It's not as big as Kurt's—few are—but a good-sized cock all the same. I curl my fingers tentatively around the shaft. It's warm and smooth and responds to my touch. I think I hear the guy in the other booth moan, but I'm not sure. It could be Kurt. It could be the performers in the porn video.

Leaning forward, I bring my tongue to the head of the anonymous cock, tasting its salty residue. My tongue caresses the tapered crown, and I feel the shaft pulse in my fist. Behind me, Kurt is pushing his lubricated dong against my puckered asshole. My dick quivers in the open air, impatient for release.

A grunt pushes its way around the cock in my mouth as

Kurt thrusts his hard rod in deep. I raise my ass to meet his downward plunge, the weight of his dick pressing against my prostate making my hard-on ache. I gulp down the anonymous prick stuffed in my mouth, hungry to taste every last inch. Still, I wish it was Kurt's cock I was sucking, wish he was cloned so I could enjoy that fantastic meatpole of his at both ends simultaneously.

Kurt rams into me, wiggling his hips so his cock twists inside my chute. My dick is really dripping now, and I take my hand away from the mystery dong and reach between my legs. I curl my fist around my shaft and my body shudders. Three strokes and I could be gushing all over the nasty floor of the viewing booth. So I keep my hand still, wanting the moment to last as long as I can manage.

The guy in the neighboring booth thrusts forward, fucking my mouth. My lips cling to that throbbing tube of flesh, my tongue presses against the swollen head. Kurt's moving very little now. He's got his cock buried all the way inside me and holds it there, keeping still, letting my ass muscles massage the veiny contours of his thick shaft.

My breathing is a roar within my ears, and all other sounds—the grunting of the man in the next booth, Kurt's moans, the stale music of the porno—are beneath it, like a separate track. Then, through the rush of my own breath I hear Kurt snarl in my ear: "Is he about to cum? You ready to swallow that hot load, baby? You like that, don't you? You're my little cum pig, aren't you?"

He's talking low, raspy and mean. It's the type of voice that would scare you to death if it came from behind on a deserted street. Other times, like now, it can get you so hot you think you might burst into flames. Unconsciously, I start pulling on my cock. I hear, "Yes, yes, yes..." and realize it's my own voice.

The mystery cock and mine erupt almost simultaneously. Tart, salty cum floods my mouth and I pull away, just in time to take another splat on my face. Kurt says, "Oh, yeah," in a low, guttural moan. I cum then. My body shakes, and I make a noise, something that sounds like a dying breath. The anonymous prick pumps out another spurt. I grab it and rub the sticky head against my face, knowing Kurt enjoys watching.

Kurt calls me a string of filthy names and pumps my ass a few more times before letting go. Even though I've spent my load, my cock still quivers as he slides in and out of my hole.

The stranger's dick retracts into the glory hole. I hear a zipper and he's gone. Kurt and I reposition ourselves so I'm sitting on Kurt's cock and facing the small TV screen. The scene has ended and all that's showing now is a static advertisement for a straight porn website.

I close my eyes and smile.

Then suddenly voices are screaming at me...hands grabbing me... I fight back... "Kurt, help me! Don't go!"

I can't feel him, see him; he's gone. I struggle with the hands pulling me from the booth, away from my lover, from his big dick and his strong arms....

Two Weeks Later

I'm sitting on a sofa that looks like a hand-me-down from the lobby of a Ramada. Plants line the windowsill and the drab green walls are decorated with diplomas and Escher prints. A heavyset woman, whose haircut accentuates the roundness of her face, sits across from me. Dr. Patricia—"Call Me Pat"—Weidler wants me to repeat my story for the hundredth goddamn time.

"You remember what you were doing? Before you were brought to…here?"

Pat doesn't like to say "hospital," as if not saying the word will help me forget I've been sent to a loony bin. I don't know what happened to Kurt. I haven't seen him since that night in the arcade. I think the cops dragged him away. They don't want me to see him. Don't they know we belong together?

I roll my eyes. At my first session with her, I was embarrassed to tell the story, and kept skirting around the details with a bashful, "You know." Now, though, I enjoy sharing every raunchy detail.

"You like that story, don't you?" I say. "Okay, again: Kurt and I went to the porno bookstore to have some fun. We went back to one of the viewing booths and…"

Pat's shaking her head. "No, that's not it at all."

"Don't tell me how it went. Kurt and I went into the booth. We were both real horny and had our cocks out before the video—"

Then she says, again: "James, there is no Kurt."

"The hell there isn't! He's been fucking me for a month! Now my parents and their homophobic lawyer have put me in this place, trying to keep us apart. 'You need a rest,' my ass! You're in on it, too, I bet. This is some sort of conversion therapy, isn't it? Christ, it all makes sense now. My parents sure didn't choose this place based on the décor. My jail cell was nicer."

Pat does her best to appear understanding, but I read her expression as one of condescending tolerance. "When the security person at the store opened the door, they found you on the floor with a…a dildo in your"—she looks out the window at the parking lot—"rectum."

"So, what are you saying?"

"I'm saying you used a sex toy to bring a fantasy to life, a fantasy that took on more meaning to you than real life."

"Bullshit! Kurt exists. I can fucking prove it. He's made movies, hundreds of them. Take me to the nearest porno store and I'll show you. You might even want to rent a few. I've read some dykes get off on guys fucking more than they do on lesbian porn."

Pat ignores my outburst. "Yes, there is a Kurt Curtis, who has made a number of adult videos," she says calmly. "Has quite a following, from what I understand. He's so popular he sells a dildo cast from his own genitals."

"So, you see!" I rest my case.

"No, don't you see? You have never met the real Kurt Curtis. All you have is a plastic replica of his penis. You have no boyfriend, James. Just a fantasy that you allowed to consume your life."

I'm silent so long that Pat says my name, concern in her voice. "James? Do you understand now? Do you understand why you were brought here?"

"Yes."

She smiles, and says I've taken an important first step. With luck, I'll be out of the hospital by the end of the month. "And ultimately, that's what we all want. You out of here and living a healthy life as soon as possible."

I nod and smile. Yes, ultimately, that's what I want, too. The sooner I'm out of here, the sooner I'm back with Kurt. I'm getting a boner just thinking about him. What do these idiots know?

SATURDAY PUNK

Bob Condron

Larry stuffed his hands deep into his pockets and headed away from Dublin town center, toward Rathmines. He needed to clear his head. A brisk walk would do the trick. Eighteen years old and in a semipermanent state of arousal. All sexed up with nowhere to go on a damp Dublin day.

Rain started spitting and the wind was up. At first Larry found it bracing, but he quickly began to wish he had brought a hat of one sort or another. His head was shaved and his skull was beginning to ache with the damp and the cold. Still he kept walking. Singing to himself, the B-side of the Clash's "White Riot." "1977...I hope I go to heaven..." Every inch the Saturday punk in his torn school blazer and bondage pants.

He had had no intention of going into the Toban Street toilets. None. But there they were just up ahead, and set back from the road. The street deserted but for a van parked opposite. On impulse, he snuck in out of the rain. One man was standing stock-still at the stalls. Larry took up position alongside him, undid his fly and stared at the wall straight ahead. No sound of pissing, no movement from either party.

The other guy must have been in his midforties, thickset and chunky, with a full, thick beard and moustache. There was nothing manicured about him. A man's man. A Garda? The bearded guy turned his head to the side almost imperceptibly and cast an eye over Larry. Larry paused, not knowing if he should risk making a move. After a moment's hesitation, he bottled out, zipped up and made his escape.

He got no more than ten feet from the exit before looking back. The burly guy had followed him out. Another ten feet, another look. The elder's eyes once again met the younger's, so Larry turned around and waited. His pursuer was over like a shot.

"Hello. How are you doing?" The man's eyes now checked Larry out from head to toe while his face split in a big, friendly grin.

"That's not a Dublin accent now?" Larry asked him.

"No. I'm up from the country. You live around here though, do you?"

"Yeah...but not on my own," Larry added quickly.

The man looked up into gray storm clouds. "I've a couple of hours to pass but the weather looks none too good."

"You're right there. Pity. I've a couple of hours to pass myself. Don't fancy getting cold and wet."

The man's eyes danced down to Larry's basket. "Would you like to go for a little drive in my van?"

"You mean now?"

Larry waited until the man looked him straight in the eye and nodded.

"Sure, why not."

They drove toward the university accompanied only by the sound of the engine and, above this, the wipers sweeping drizzle from the windscreen. It gave Larry the opportunity to size up his companion. His hair was cut fairly short but tousled, curly and sandy blond. The hands that clutched the wheel were bigger than average, as were his feet. *Big feet, big meat?* thought Larry, and smiled to himself. The man wore heavy brown boots, brown corduroy trousers, a brown checked shirt and had big, brown eyes to match. He put Larry in mind of a woolly mammoth. Big and strong and tough, a throwback to some former time. Yeah, he would do; he would do very nicely.

The campus grounds were quiet on a weekend even at the best of times, but on this rain-gray afternoon they were totally deserted. The man parked near a quiet wooded spot and, fixing the hand brake with one swift hand movement, let go one knob and clutched another—Larry's. Purposefully, he rubbed Larry's fly. Larry sighed and as the air eased out of his lungs the blood rushed into his dick. Stiff and swollen in moments, his mickey throbbed as the stranger worked his fingers deep into the grooves of Larry's bulge.

"I bet you've got a right big cock on you. I bet you've got a big, fat mickey," the man chuckled, lustily.

"Take it out and see for yourself," Larry urged him.

"In the back." He tipped back his head in the direction of the rear of the van. "More room to get comfortable." The man already had the driver's door halfway open.

Outside, the stranger threw wide the double doors at the back of the van to reveal a makeshift bed; foam cushions covered by a blanket. Larry put one foot up to climb in and the man cupped both his buttocks, hoisting him over the threshold. Larry landed facedown. Climbing in behind him, the man pulled the doors shut and fastened them securely. Pitch black. Then he flicked the switch on some kind of portable lamp. The stranger's face was flushed and glistened in the yellowish glow.

Larry flipped over onto his back and relaxed, his hands behind his head, as the man knelt over him. The stranger's fingers fumbled with Larry's belt buckle and the button on the waist of his jeans, then trembled as they tugged the zip down over the pronounced curvature of Larry's bulge. No underwear meant all obstacles had been removed and Larry's cock burst forth.

The man chuckled, "I'd have won that bet! Fuck! Will you look at the size of that! What a beauty!" His thick fingers now encircled Larry's pulsing girth and retracted the heavy coverlet of foreskin. Helmet of Larry's cock exposed, the stranger lowered his salivating mouth slowly down.

The man hesitated, eyes closed, wet tongue half hanging out, and then he dipped the pointed tip into Larry's drooling piss slit. Lapping up the clear, sparkling juice, he savored it in much the same way a connoisseur of fine wine might test the first sip from a fresh bottle. Then, reverently, he kissed the lips of Larry's knob, allowing his own to part and slide over it. Lips fixed around the rim, he sucked for a while, taking time to unbutton his own fly and yank free his distended organ. Clasping it in his fist, he began to jerk the foreskin back and forth, back and forth.

It was raining heavily now, pounding on the metal roof above their heads. Inside, the van smelt of the country, of straw and earth. The stranger's mouth worked up and down the full length of Larry's shaft, relaxing his throat to embrace him fully. Sensations of pleasure rippled through Larry's entire body as the man's beard tickled his balls. He clasped the back of the stranger's head and let his hand rest there, moving in rhythm as the stranger's eager mouth plunged forward and back.

This guy is desperate, thought Larry, but it was a desperation that delighted him. The man was cock hungry, and Larry's dick was the sole focus of his ravenous and seemingly insatiable appetite. Something profound struck Larry as he looked down upon the rapturous expression on the man's face. His need was primal. Sucking cock was as basic and fundamental to him as the need to breathe or eat or piss.

Now the stranger was whining through lips clamped tight around Larry's member. Larry knew he couldn't hold off much longer, even if he had wanted to.

"I'm close...close to coming."

The man pulled back and gasped, "Can I swallow you?"

"Yeah...yeah...just don't fuckin' stop."

Massaging Larry's bollocks, the man redoubled his efforts—moaning with his mouth full, clobbering on his own dick, urging Larry to come. A searing white light flashed before Larry's eyes as aching balls lifted to expel his payload. The stranger gulped and snaffled and squeezed the juice from Larry's plums. Larry's body convulsed and his cock continued to spasm. The man hungrily consumed every drop, and continued to suck on Larry's softening tool as he pumped his own, whilst his other hand clutched his own balls and tugged. He was whimpering as his lips held on to Larry's dick. Larry raised himself up on his elbows. He reached forward and unbuttoned the man's shirt and let his fingers swirl over the man's hairy chest before finding his nipples. The stranger let out a squeal as Larry tweaked on an erect node. A moment later, the first arch of boiling lava sprayed the blanket. Then a second spurt, a third, a fourth.

Cum was everywhere. Over his hand, over the blanket, and most of it over Larry, soaking into his clothes. He really didn't care. Exhausted, the man collapsed down beside him and Larry hugged him.

"That was fucking beautiful," the stranger said, rubbing his beard over Larry's cheek. "Fuckin' beautiful!"

Larry took the man's hand and licked up the sperm from gnarled skin, tough as leather. "Are you a laborer?" he asked.

"Farmer," the man replied.

The stranger had sucked Larry's cock and Larry didn't even know his name. Now, in the comfort of Larry's arms, he let loose his intimacy.

"Are you married then?" the man asked.

"Nah. Why?"

"Only you said you didn't live alone."

"Oh, that." Larry thought quickly. "I share with a mate." It was a lie born out of necessity. He could hardly tell this big bruiser that he still lived at home with his mammy.

"A mate you fuck with?"

"And then some!" One lie begetting another.

"Lucky young bastard! Thought you were too young to be married. How old are you?"

"Not so young. Twenty-one." He was getting good at this. The man sighed. "It's a good age."

"And are you married?"

"With ten kids."

"Ten!"

"Had the first three by the time I was twenty-one."

Silence. "And how long have you been...having sex with men?"

"Long before. But we didn't talk about such things back then. Didn't give it a name. No one knows about this...side of me."

"You must feel pretty isolated?"

"You're not wrong there."

The man held tight on to Larry. For the longest while, or so it seemed, they kissed and cuddled like a courting couple. Eventually, the stranger said it was time to make a move.

On impulse, Larry reached into his blazer pocket, producing a scrap of paper and a pen. He scribbled his name and address and handed it over. "In case you want to keep in touch."

The stranger looked at the scrap of paper for a long moment. "My name's Liam, by the way." He folded the scrap, stuffed it in his shirt pocket, and said, with a melancholy air, "Seeing you again would be grand but it just might make things a wee bit too complicated."

The clinic was down a back street. Hidden away from prying eyes. Larry had made an appointment but still had to take a seat and sweat.

"The doctor will see you shortly," said a starched nurse with all the warmth and understanding of a fridge-freezer.

Larry felt sick.

First, the irritating itch began under the foreskin, then the rash had appeared shortly after. A rash of tiny red pimples across his cockhead. Where did he get them from? The possibilities seemed endless—he had been putting it about a bit. Had he got it from the farmer or given it to him? Shit! Shit! Shit!

"The doctor will see you now," grunted Nurse Face-Ache. "Go down the hall, first room on your right."

"Thanks," Larry replied, with no conviction.

He entered the room to find a woman doctor, hair pulled back in a severe bun, black plastic half-moon glasses perched on the end of her nose. She was seated behind a desk. As he approached she looked up from a chart and smiled. At least her face was kindly. She must be used to abject terror in her line of work, Larry thought.

"Take a seat," she said. "Now, what's the problem?"

He explained the symptoms and she said, "We had better have a little look."

Usually, he would have had no problem presenting his pride and joy for inspection—but in these circumstances? It was excruciating! He pulled back the foreskin and waited to be told the worst. She examined it, then, raising her eyebrows, she looked directly into his eyes.

"Nothing to worry about, Mr.—" She checked her register. "—er...Smith. It's just a little touch of beard rash."

from BILL IN EXILE

C. Scott Smith and William Meloyd Cullum

The following correspondence is excerpted
from a collection of letters exchanged between
Bill (my best friend) and me (Scott) while Bill
is locked up in prison for selling methamphetamine to upper-middle-class gay white boys in
New York City. I wrote the Bill in Exile entries, Bill wrote the Posts from the Joint; they
were posted on the blog Bill in Exile beginning
in January 2005. The letters, and by extension
the blog, are nothing more than a continuation
of the conversation that Bill and I have been
having with each other for almost twenty-five
years.

Feb. 3, 2005: Bill in Exile #13—Fucking Private Ryan
Dear Bill,

Ski, my buddy from the Marines, was a real piece of work...
how is it, with you having AIDS on the brain since like 1983
and being a low-life degenerate drug addict for even longer,
that you can remember shit like that? It's a wonderment!

But you reminding me of Ski in turn reminded me of a time
in the Marines when he decided he was going to get me laid
with this absolutely drop-dead boy named Private First Class
Johnny Ryan (not his real name, for reasons that will be clear
to you later). We were at Camp Fuji on the slopes of Mt. Fuji
on mainland Japan, and my infantry company was going to do
a thirty-mile night forced march around part of the mountain,
and at the end of the march we were going to bivouac (that's
military talk for camp out).

Each man in an infantry platoon (thirty-six, approximately)
is issued what's known as a shelter half, which is one half of a
pup tent; you're supposed to buddy up with another Jarhead
in order to combine the two halves and make a tent that two
can sleep in. Before the march kicked off my platoon got tem-
porarily assigned a new guy—Johnny Ryan. He was an anti-
tank gunner and his assignment as a temp meant he didn't have
anyone to "hooch" with. I was the platoon sergeant, having
just been bumped up to that job from squad leader after our
old platoon sergeant, Sgt. Head (real name, I swear to god!)
got caught giving a little of the same, head that is, to another
grunt, and got his butt slung in the brig.

Anyway, I was the senior enlisted man in the platoon, so it
fell to me to hooch with new guy, Johnny—just about the most
smokin' hot beautiful blond boy from the woods of South
Carolina. Over six feet tall, with big wide shoulders from

slinging hay on some sharecropper's farm no doubt, pouty lips, and these insane sapphire blue eyes with gold streaks. Plus, he was underage when he went to enlist, and had to have his parents sign over his guardianship to the Marines. He was all of seventeen years old on the day he reported to my platoon, and I'm pretty sure it was right about then that I developed my taste for chicken. I was a grizzled veteran of twenty-two. Ryan reports for duty and Ski recognizes immediately that he is a potential target of opportunity for me, but he knows that I am way too shy to do anything about it on my own. Also, just recently having Sgt. Head locked up for buggery would probably keep me from moving on Ryan, and Ski knew this. So Ski announces to Ryan and the rest of the platoon before we step off that since Ryan has drawn the lot to hooch with me, and since it's his first time with first platoon, he has to comply with the first platoon tradition: that every Marine who hooches with the platoon sergeant for the first time has to put out.

Needless to say, everyone in the platoon thought this was hysterical, even Ryan at first, but First Platoon Kilo Company 3rd Battalion 2nd Marines had been together for over a year and a half at that point and we all knew each other's moves by heart, and at this instigation by Ski the platoon became like a bunch of sharks that had just been chummed. They saw what Ski had in mind and they went for poor Ryan like he was a baitfish. For the entire forced march they were saying shit like, "Oh Johnny, you better limber up that hole." "Johnny gonna give some poop chute tonight." "Hey Ryan, you love me long time GI?" They actually started calling him "Johnny-poo." You know, the usual kind of harassment that barely postado-lescent boys perpetrate upon one another when they spend too much time together in close proximity, while simultaneously

possessed of raging hormones and encouraged by their supe-
riors to display extreme aggression at all times—and carry au-
tomatic weapons when they go to work. By the end of the
forced march, Johnny was acting a bit frazzled and squirrelly
and I'm sure that I was starting to look to the poor boy like a
big dangerous spider just waiting for the next meal—and he
just knew that he and his stellar ass had been cast by Ski in the
role of the fly.

So we finish the hump around sunrise and it's getting ready
to rain its ass off and we put up our tents and everyone is just
fucking dog-assed tired. I get in the tent and Ryan climbs in
after me and I'm on my side with my head propped up in my
hand facing him and Ryan gets all settled to go to sleep and
just as he closes his eyes I say, "So how 'bout it, junior?" You
could just about hear that poor boy's eyelids snap open. He
goes, "How 'bout what?" in that lovely South Carolina drawl.
I said, "You know the platoon rule. First time you hooch with
me you gotta put out."

"Oh man," he said, "I thought you guys was jes' fuckin'
with me." I said: "Oh no, we were dead serious. You gotta
put out." At this point you could hear something like terror
in his voice when he said again, "But I thought y'all was jes'
fuckin' with me. 'Sides, I never done nuthin' like that before."
By now it was getting really blowy outside and the rain was
just starting and I said, "Look Ryan, I'm gonna give you ten
seconds to think about it. If by the time I count down from ten
you haven't decided to put out then you can get the fuck out
and sleep in the rain." So I start counting from ten and don't
you know that somewhere around six or seven I just fell flat
asleep? Next thing I know I'm being shaken awake, and as
I'm doing the old wha? who's there? Ryan says to me, in what

is a much huskier sounding voice, with just a bit of very sexy tremolo to it, "Okay sir, I'll put out."

Bingo. Man, I was wide fucking awake in a half a heartbeat, and you could cut the sexual tension in that tent with a knife. It took me all of a fucking nanosecond to get us both out of our uniforms, and just after I rolled him over on his stomach he looks back over his shoulder at me with these huge fucking blue/gold eyes and whispers, "Ya'll kin fuck me up the ass, sir, but ya cain't kiss me 'cause that'll make me kwaar." Translation: Please fuck me daddy but don't kiss me because if you do that it will just confirm to me that I am a huge fucking homosexual.

So Johnny boy got boinked on the black volcanic ash slope of Mt. Fuji early that morning, with it thundering and raining like a motherfucker outside, and he got boinked many other mornings and evenings thereafter. He became quite the dirty little boy of Kilo company, and even got over his fear of being turned "kwaar" by kissing. One time on leave in Tokyo he ran out of money and couldn't get home and even tried to whore himself out to me. He asked me to loan him some cash for the train and added, as a sweetener I guess, "If ya'll loan me the money I'll let ya do whatever ya'll want to me, sir." I said, "Johnny, here's your train money, son, and in case you haven't noticed, I already do whatever the fuck I want to you."

"Johnny Ryan" was a true beauty, a great kid, and most importantly, a good Marine. He was blown to pieces along with 219 of his brother Marines and 21 other American servicemen on October 23, 1983 at the Marine Barracks in Beirut, Lebanon.

Scott

May 12, 2005: A Post from the Joint
Dear Scott,

I was thrilled to hear from you that a large number of people who are stumbling upon the blog are doing so by way of searches undertaken in order to satisfy any number of perversions and strange fetishes. I particularly liked the "ahhh, dentist touched sensitive cavity on tooth" search. Can't you just imagine who this person is? Probably sitting in front of a computer in a dark room, naked and covered in lube from jacking off while IMing other preverts and looking at exchanged pics of various PREversions. His keyboard is probably ruined it's got so much lube caked on it—and as I'm writing this I'm realizing that I'm describing what a person looks like who has been tweaking on meth for about three or four days. Been there, done that! Thinking about this, though, got me thinking about fetishes in general and how people develop them and then satisfy them and why; really is interesting until, that is, it gets creepy, which most times is exactly what they become.

I remember meeting this one guy at that sex club down on Houston Street a couple of years ago, Club El Mirage. Don't you just love that name? Joel what's-his-name who owned it was such a pretentious twit that he wanted to name his club with a Euro-sounding name but he was so fuckin' dumb that he mixed French and Spanish together. Oh well, you don't need a degree in nuclear physics to run a sex club, I guess. Anyway, I remember I was sitting in the lounge having a cigarette and watching these two fairly nice-looking boys take turns eating each other's asses when this plain-looking guy sat down to remove his street clothes. We said hi and it wasn't until he started to get out of his underwear that I noticed he was jingling like a reindeer. I thought it was keys at first, but then when he was full-on naked and still jingling I took a close look and his cock and balls looked like a piece of mid-gothic-period chain mail. He was so heavily pierced that you couldn't see any skin.

I complimented him on his piercings and he nodded his thanks and said something like, "Yes, I've got twenty-six scrotal piercings and thirty-two penile piercings, not including the Prince Alberts, which I run multiple rings and studs through a single hole and then like to hang heavy weights from. I've also got my frenum heavily pierced."

He bent over and showed me his butthole; it looked like something that U.S. Steel had put together for a display of their products. I was really amazed by it all and started asking him what got him into it and why he had taken it so far and his response was, "You know, I got my first piercing, a Prince Albert, years ago and it was like eating potato chips for me. I couldn't stop even if I wanted to. I just kept going back for more and more."

We talked for a bit before Joel, the owner, came over to speak with him, "So although it's obvious I'm into piercing, that's not really my 'thing' anymore," he told Joel. (Yes, Scott he did make hand "quotes," since I'm sure you're wondering, and I just know how that would make you crawl out of your skin even more than almost fifty cock piercings.) "What I'm really into is ritual cutting, where I'm the cutter, and the use of sounds, and also catheterization. I'm happy to act as the top doing that but I'd much rather be catheterized by someone else. Do you think that I'll be able to find anyone with the same interests here?"

"I'm sure you can, dear," Joel told him. "And if you can't, I'll get my boyfriend Stevie to put a tube up your urethra, since he's studying to be an ultrasound tech. It's practically the same isn't it?"

The guy wasn't too sure of that, but he said he thought it might be okay. Then, he opened his trick bag and pulled out about four feet of surgical tubing with a butterfly clamp on one end, and proceeded to insert the open end into the head of his dick and down (or up) his urethra. Well, let me tell you. That got absolutely everyone's attention in that lounge, even the boys who were heavily involved in their own little ass-munching. Once the tube was about two or so feet in, he turned the valve open and a stream of piss shot down the tube and out onto the floor. Not much, just a spurt before he closed the valve, but now the tube was filled with piss. He took out a roll of surgical tape and taped the tube up the side of his torso to just below his underarm with the tube and valve pointing out front past his left pec about three inches. I looked at him quizzically and almost immediately he said, "In case someone wants a drink."

Duh! Stupid me. Then he pulled a pretty black leather case out of his trick bag and opened it up and inside on a red velvet lining were about twenty sounds (those surgical probes for examining body cavities) of all different lengths and gauges. He also pulled out a magnet that looked as if it weighed about three pounds. My curiosity about this was evident, I guess, because he looked at me and said, "I really like having someone insert sounds up my urethra and then once one of the big ones is in place, use the magnet to move it up and down inside my cock. It's a little twist that I added that's sort of my own touch—a signature move like one of Michael Jordan's front fist pumps after a slam dunk."

At this point it started to dawn on me what this guy's fetishes were really all about. They were about showing off. It was sort of like watching a little kid at the playground jumping up and down and screaming, "Look at me, look at me," over and over. He also had some really nice-looking and what turned out to be antique surgical scalpels of varying sizes that he said he liked to use for ritual cutting. I suggested that flowing blood products might be a problem for the club, but Joel chimed in immediately, "Oh, don't worry, we'll clean up any mess you make."

I saw him later that night on a padded table in the main room inserting long metal sounds up his cock and moving them up and down with the aid of his powerful magnet to the sounds of ABBA on the club sound system. He looked quite content and he had an audience, which I'm sure made him even happier.

I'm going to lunch. I miss you.

Bill

May 13, 2005: Bill in Exile #57—Fetish Obsessives
Dear Bill,

Your letter yesterday about the fetish obsessive you observed at Club El Mirage was hysterical and quite timely, since we were out at dinner the night before last with our buddy Mel and he was telling us about this guy he knows in L.A. who was a collector of male pubic hair. But not pubic hair from any old area or place. Pubic hair that he was able to retrieve from the urinals in public men's rooms. "Public pubic hair," you might call it. Like your fetish obsessive with the multiple piercings, Mel's friend started out with a sort of generalized fetish for public loos that he then fine-tuned into a real narrowly focused obsession with collecting pubic hair that had been deposited on the urinals in the bathrooms. Mel said that he had these fishing tackle-like boxes, the kind with lots and lots of compartments and levels, and all of the compartments had different types of pubes in little plastic Ziplock bags, all marked with date, time, and place, including a small cross-indexed card to describe the man whose hair it was, if that was information known to the collector. Creepy, no?

Kisses,

Scott

May 26, 2005: A Post from the Joint

Dear Scott,

OMG. I just read your letter #57 to me about fetish obsessives; that guy your friend Mel described, who collected pubic hair, reminded me of these two scat queens I met once. They were boyfriends, and one was a lawyer and the other was an accountant or some shit. Leave it to lawyers and accountants to have the most disgusting fetishes. Anyway, they were both really hardcore scat queens and would usually have to hire hookers to fulfill their needs, since most other people they would meet would run screaming from them. They were referred to me, and I went over to their apartment for a job—and as soon as I got to their apartment they handed me $250 and said I'd get another $250 when I left, and then they handed me a big Ziplock bag and told me to go into their powder room and take a dump.

I didn't have to have sex with them, or even get undressed; all I had to do was take a shit. When I was done I was chatting with them about their fetish and I was pretending to be interested, for as you know I like to collect information about stuff that I don't know much about, and scat was definitely one of those things. Once I had made them feel comfortable, they took me into their kitchen to show me their "collection." They had one of those freezers with the door on top. Inside that big chest were like 100 or more freezer bags just like the one I had filled for them, and all of them were dated and had a brief description on a plastic card attached to the bag of who the "supplier" was, what he looked like, and a comment or two. It made my head spin to think about these two dorks sitting around indexing and cross-indexing their collection of turds, like they were baseball cards or something. Then I started to think about what they did with them once the indexing was all done and I decided it was time for me to leave.

Bill

May 29, 2005: A Post from the Joint

Dear Scott,

One of my homo buddies here in the joint and I were chatting about porno the other day. This guy William has an encyclopedic knowledge of gay porn. Anyway, I was telling him that you had a history of dating/doing porno stars and he wanted to know which ones, so as I was going through your CV of porn stars I came to that unbelievably beautiful boy that you sent over to my place so I could photograph him. But for the life of me I haven't been able to remember his name. He was Latin but with some Russian-sounding name, and when I photographed him he had just had a big movie released and a big spread in *Advocate Men* that was really hot. Do you know who I'm talking about here? God! I hate getting old and not being able to remember shit like this.

My new cell/cube mate, Mike the Nazi, has been "educating" me on the finer points of white supremacy, and I've been finding the subject to be highly entertaining. They seem to have a sliding scale for their hatred; various groups and ethnicities garner differing degrees of contempt from them. According to Mike the Nazi, "niggers" are obviously the worst since one can readily see their depraved and subhuman condition by the color of their skin. "Chinks" the same, except that they seem to be a bit higher on the food chain than blacks because they are "hard workers and bring up real estate values" in the neighborhoods they move into, as Mike the Nazi helpfully explained to me. Jews are obviously reviled because they are dirty moneylenders and Christ killers, but Mike the Nazi does seem to have a dirty little secret that the rest of his Aryan Nation boys here at the prison don't know about—that he once had sex with a "filthy little Jewess," as he put it, but said it was the best sex he had ever had. I told him about you and that you had a bit of a history with Jewish boys and always said that they were great sex and usually had really big dicks to boot. Mike the Nazi tried to look sickened by this news, but I could tell he was more than a little titillated. Don't you just imagine that every good little Nazi secretly wants to be ravaged and penetrated by some subhuman? Some dirty circumcised *untermenchen*? I know I do!

OMG! I just remembered his name. Carlos Morales, that was the porno star you used to date that I brain farted the name of. Remember him? What a beauty! When he came over to my studio he completely took my breath away. I couldn't believe you were doing him at the time. How did you hook up with him?

So anyway, I'm learning a lot about the neo-Nazi movement here in America and I gotta tell you, if they all didn't seem to be so fucking stupid I might be worried about them. It's really amazing how you can take a fairly straightforward message of hate and xenophobia, sprinkle it with some biblical passages and presto—every stupid fuck with an IQ hovering around 85 who's ever felt as if he's been put upon by someone who isn't lily white is ready to buy in. These guys would be laughably tragic were it not for the fact that when they get hold of firearms they tend to want to use them on people. The one saving grace in all this is that as many profoundly stupid people as there are in this country, you would think that the neo-Nazi message would get more traction than it does, but the fact that it does not, I think, is testament to the even more extreme level of stupidity displayed by its supporters. Most of these guys couldn't organize their way to a normal bowel movement schedule without outside help, so getting a nice big group of people together to *Seig Heil* with on the weekends seems to be beyond their abilities altogether.

Love,
Bill

May 31, 2005: Bill in Exile #65—Carlos Morales, Porn Star
Dear Bill,

His Nom de Porn is indeed Carlos Morales and yes, I guess you could say he's got a Russian-sounding real first name, since it's Ivan, but as you are aware, that's also a Latin first name and Carlos/Ivan is most definitely Latin, and possessed of all the passion implied by his ethnicity—as well as an enormous fucking dollop of sleaze, as one would hope of a porn star.

We met at the Hangar on Christopher Street of all places. From time to time the Hangar would bring in go-go dancers to dance at the back of the bar and although having dancers in a tiny shithole like the Hangar may seem a bit much it was a nice break from the gay pool tournaments and happy hours complete with soggy baked chicken tenders and cheese platters of greasy cheddar and greasier pepperoni slices that they usually tried to push off on their customers.

My shitbag ex-business partner Jay used to adore going to the Hangar, for as you recall, Jay has a real thing for big streety black men, especially if there exists a definite possibility that he might get robbed or have the shit kicked out of him after doing the nasty with them. Such is the depth of Jay's depravity, and the Hangar was fully up to the task of providing Jay with just what he was looking for. Jay used to stop by my apartment on Christopher Street for a warm-up cocktail and then he and I would head down to the Hangar for happy hour, since in addition to having an affinity for flirting with danger Jay was/is one of the world's most low-down cheap-assed skinflints and would only go to bars when two-for-one was in effect.

Anyway, I digress... so Jay and I had gone to the Hangar for happy hour and that day was a go-go boy day and dancing at the back of the bar was none other than Carlos Morales. As you know full well, Bill, I have always had a thing for hot go-go boys, having made a point of hooking up with as many as I could over the years, and as you also well know, I have an even bigger thing for porn stars. I parked myself right at the back of the bar near his box and proceeded to have meaningful eye contact with him. Now my idea of meaningful eye contact was something quite sophisticated and very Cary Grantesque; however, I suspect that the reality was more grotesque than Grantesque, since I probably looked like a bitch dog in heat. But whatever I was doing it seemed to have a salutary effect, for as his set ended Carlos jumped off his box and, wearing only his electric green banana hammock, tennis shoes, and a thin sheen of sweat, came over to me and asked me my name. I told him and he said, "I've got one more half-hour set. Whatever you do, don't leave."

Carlos headed back to his go-go box to finish his set, and a half hour later joined me after changing into his street clothes. He said he was really sweaty from dancing and I asked him if he wanted to take a shower at my place, which as a pickup line may seem a bit odd—but since he had already picked me up, I figured what the fuck. He thought that was a great idea, so we left Jay to his thugz and headed back to my apartment half a block away.

When we arrived I set Carlos up in the shower and told him I'd make us a couple of cocktails. He asked if I had anything comfortable he could wear and I pointed out the dresser in the bedroom to him and told him to help himself to anything he liked. As I finished pouring the drinks Carlos came into the living room, and apparently his idea of comfortable clothing and what I was thinking were a bit different—though what he had chosen was perfectly fine if you asked me. He had forgone the gym shorts and T-shirts drawer and found the leather and latex drawer instead; he was wearing a skintight pair of rubberized chaps by Nasty Pig. He also wore a classic black jock by Bike that had gotten a lot of mileage over the years, and was as comfortable as I imagine an old cardigan sweater would be, if I had ever worn one. On his feet: a pair of black leather lace-up lineman boots by Wesco that I had gotten at Stompers in San Francisco. I'm giving you the labels here, Bill, so you can experience some of the flavor of what Carlos was wearing—but also because I'm a label queen.

One of the things about Carlos that doesn't come across in

film is that he is absolutely covered in freckles. They are really pale *café au lait* and don't show up all that well on film, which is tragic, but in person they are seriously spectacular. So standing in a jock and rubber chaps and boots in my living room was this freckled porn star who was, I might add, filling out my jock more and more as I stared at him. Once I had recovered from my initial sight of him, I pulled myself together sufficiently to lay on him one of my all-time tried and true compliments/come-ons.

"Wow," I said.

Okay, okay, I know! But give me a fucking break here, it's Carlos fucking Morales *and* he's wearing rubber chaps and a jock in my living room and at this point I'm pretty sure I'm gonna get laid so you can understand my being at a loss for words.

As he executed a slow 360 for me to check out the merch, he said, "I thought you might like me in this more than sweatpants and a T-shirt. I hope you don't mind."

"Wow," I said again, but this time was able to follow that up with, "Your ass looks so fucking incredible in those chaps, I'm having a little trouble breathing."

He smiled and walked over to me and, taking the drinks from my hands, kneeled in front of me and, as he unzipped my jeans, looked up and smiled. "Thanks." Then: "Most people think that just because I've got a big cock I'm a top, and as soon as I pull it out even guys who were planning on fucking me want to put their asses in the air for me. But as much as I love to fuck, I'm really a bottom at heart. I hope that's not going to be a problem for you."

"I'll figure out a way to manage," I said.

He and I had a lot of fun together that day and many other

days thereafter. We discovered that with a couple of exceptions (scat being one of them, for as you know I firmly believe that "shit is not sexy"), there was very little that either one of us would not try and we each took a great deal of glee in introducing the other to new "perversions." But as fun as the sex with him was, the thing that I will always remember is what an absolute sweetheart he is. Ivan/Carlos Morales is just one of those people who are so genuinely nice it takes your breath away. Kinda like his ass.

So that was how I met Carlos Morales.

Later,

Scott

June 14, 2005: A Post from the Joint

Dear Scott,

I've met a couple of guys who seem to be possible buddies. One is a meth dealer doing a dime. He got popped for a couple of ounces, thus the ten-year sentence. His name is Joey and he's about twenty-two and cute in that sort of dazed and confused look that all meth dealers acquire if they do too much of their own product. He looks kind of like Fez from *That '70s Show* and has a big old fat uncut dick that I couldn't keep my eyes off of in the shower the other day. He totally caught me and just smiled and kept on lathering it up for me until it started to look like a baby's arm holding an apple with a shower cap on. I had to flee the shower before I got a boner. Do you think that makes me a big homo?

Anyway, Joey is definitely a big homo, and he's told me about his prison conquests. It's funny, he's found that if you lock a bunch of guys in a facility together and don't allow them the pleasures of female company, not only will the gay guys gravitate to the guys with big cocks, but so will the straight guys. Joey and I "walk the track" together every evening after dinner, and he likes to point out the guys he's fucked since he's been here. Normally I would take his stories with a grain of salt, but whenever he says hello to the straight guys he says he's fucked, they get all nervous like they've got a secret that they don't want him telling. He told me that he baits them into letting him fuck them by offering them blow jobs and when they get all worked up he won't let them cum until he's played with their buttholes for a while. Most always let him fuck them once he's gotten a finger inside. Well you know, once you've done that it's but a matter of time before you get them begging for something bigger, straight or not.

Bill

Dec. 1, 2005: A Post from the Joint

Dear Scott,

Well, having spent the better part of Thanksgiving Day with my wonderful parents who came to visit me (for the first time ever and after my being in prison for over a year), I am pretty sure that after I finish this letter to you I'm going to attempt to drown myself in one of the toilets that I just finished cleaning. The visit was everything I expected and then some.

A little background on this first: As you know, my parents are essentially clueless, awful people. Dad never met a child that he couldn't "fix" with beatings that could devolve to broken bones and hospital visits, and Mom dealt with Dad's violence by believing he was somehow acting as the right arm of God and that he was serving as the "Lord's scourge" when he tortured his children. She didn't like the violence but her place was at her husband's side and her job was to support him and his job was to beat Satan out of us kids even if it meant killing one of us.

Now, having provided this background, don't get me wrong. As you know, I've never once blamed them for what I became or what I did in my life. That's all on me and I take full responsibility for it good or bad. I blame them for what they did to us when they did it, period. But I've been willing to move on from there. I admit that I hated them for years, and I don't care for them now, but that's just because they are hateful people. For years though, even though I hated them, I was hugely conflicted since they are my parents, and kids, no matter how ill treated, need the love of their parents and want to love them in return.

So they came to visit, and it was just awful. They had no idea how prison worked and didn't care enough to find out before they showed up; after going through all the security checks and searches Dad was really pissed and feeling very put out, which he tried to take out on me.

"You coulda at least warned us ahead a time that these here niggers would want to be layin' their hands all over us," he snarled in that charming way that dyed in the wool racists have of speaking. I wasn't having it, though, and told him to shut his fucking mouth or he could go wait out in the car until Mom and I were done with our visit, and if he had a problem with that I'd have one of "these here niggers" remove him. By force if necessary.

That effectively ended Dad's visit with me; he simply sat for the next three hours, while Mom and I talked, occasionally chiming in with a derisive snort or a roll of the eyes, but not much more since I am sure he was mortally afraid of having one of the black COs lay his black hands on Dad's lily-white and racially pure body.

For Mom's part it was pretty much business as usual. Tears, recrimination, prayers, more tears, more prayer, blah, blah, blah. I particularly liked the point at which she announced to me that it was clear to her that God had abandoned me and that regardless of what I did in the future to try to get back in His good graces the only thing I had to look forward to was an eternity in the fires of hell.

The one good thing that may have come from the visit is that just before they left Mom hesitantly asked me why I had asked them to send money. As you know, Scott, you and my brother and Andrew C. are the only people who ever send me money or mail…and without money, even if it's just the $300 a month we are allowed for clothing, toothpaste and our phone cards and postage stamps, life goes from being bad to being really quite hellish.

So when Mom asked me, "About this money thing, since you're in prison your father and I don't understand what need you could possibly have for money. Unless you're using it to buy illicit drugs and such."

I was ready for this question, and as she asked it I smiled a sort of pitiful smile and said, "Mom, you need money in here to buy protection. If you don't pay people off, they kill you." And then I looked at my dad and said, "Or worse Dad, one of the gangs of 'niggers' that you're so afraid of will drag you into the bathroom and gang-rape you with their big black cocks and then when they're done having their way with you they'll slit your throat from ear to ear." He turned white as a sheet and honest to god started to sweat when I said that.

After that they couldn't get out of there fast enough. They might not ever send me a dime as long as I'm here and I can pretty much guarantee they won't ever visit again, but the image of my father dreaming at night about being gang-fucked by a group of sweaty black men, all with much bigger dicks than him, made the entire visit worth it.

Happy Thanksgiving,

Bill

Dec. 15, 2005: A Post from the Joint

Dear Scott,

So Trig, my Kentucky fuck buddy with the gargantuan cock, was shipped out to the federal prison outside of Lexington, Kentucky yesterday. They came during the night and woke him up so when I got up he was gone. No chance to even say good-bye. Oh well, that's how things go here. We knew his transfer date was coming up fast, although we didn't know when it was going to actually happen, so we had already said our good-byes two days before. It was sweet too. We went up to our fuck den over the chapel and he fucked me so hard I thought my eyes were going to bleed. When he dumped his load into me and after I came he didn't pull out and get dressed real fast the way he usually does and he left his fat cock in me and lay down behind me and wrapped his arms around me. And guess what? We fucking fell asleep like that. I guess we slept for almost an hour and I've got to tell you, Scott, it was the best hour's sleep I've gotten in over a year! I didn't even mind when I woke up and found that Trig was drooling on my face while he slept.

Anyway, so that's that. I guess I need to find a new fuck buddy, huh?

Bill

Dec. 22, 2005: Bill in Exile #138—The Glory Hole
Dear Bill,

Did I ever tell you about the first time I experienced the joys of a glory hole?

The amazing thing, and I know you'll find this hard to believe, was that my first time in a glory hole was not in some sleazy New York or San Francisco sex club or some public bathroom in a filthy subway station but was, in fact, in a glory hole discovered by me when I was in college. Who would have thought that Kenyon College in the sleepy town of Gambier, Ohio would have had a glory hole? And what a glory hole it was.

To say that I "discovered" this glory hole is actually misleading, since I would probably have gone four years without knowing there was one on campus were it not for my football teammate, fuck buddy and object of my jockstrap obsession, Rick Young.

Rick was lounging on the sofa in my room, having just dumped one of his enormous loads down my throat, and was sprawled out naked and idly squeezing the last drops of cum from his fat cock as I was putting on a pair of jeans and a T-shirt with the intention of heading over to the library to do some research on a paper I had due. I'm pretty sure it was a Classics paper ("Rome's Rise to World Dominance") and I'm also pretty sure I had not yet started it even though it was due the next day.

As I threw on a pair of sneakers, Rick, admiring the fine quality of his cum between his thumb and index finger said, "Stay out of the glory hole at the library if you intend to ever get that paper finished."

To say that my ears pricked up would be an understatement, and I immediately demanded to know what Rick was talking about. He told me that in the rabbit warren of study carrels on the third floor between the old library building and the new annex there was a men's room hidden off one of the hallways and in that men's room was what Rick described as a "fairly active glory hole." Well, that information practically had me sprinting to the library and after staking out a table for my research I decided to go find this glory hole Rick had told me about.

Sure enough, at the back of a dark 100-year-old hallway lined with study carrels for seniors, was a men's room that I had had no idea existed. I walked in with my heart pounding and as soon as I got into the dimly lit room I could see that two of the three stalls immediately to my front and facing the door were occupied, and from them was coming the distinct sound of a blow job being administered.

As soon as I saw this I headed to the vacant stall on the far left, walked in and closed the door, and saw a circular hole about eight to ten inches in diameter right where the toilet paper dispenser should have been. Amazingly, this hole had been padded all around with what turned out to be some kind of foam wrapped in silver duct tape. After closing and locking the stall door I sat down on the toilet to get my bearings, and not three seconds had gone by before a hand popped through the hole with its fingers waggling at me. I stood, pulled out my cock and balls, faced the partition, positioned myself so that my nuts were over the waggling fingers, and slowly lowered my balls into the hand while holding on to the top of the partition with both hands.

The hand that had come through from the center stall massaged my nuts for a minute or two before moving up to my cock, which was pressed flat against the steel partition wall above the hole. I pressed my balls in toward the hole and whoever was on the other side got his mouth right up to it, gently pulled my balls through the hole and started licking my nuts. I started moaning softly, since I love to have my balls licked, and the hand finally grabbed my cock and pulled it into his side of the stall and into his mouth.

The guy in the other stall blew me for a couple of minutes but obviously whoever was in the far stall was getting antsy, what with all the attention I was getting, and soon enough I heard a voice from the occupant of that stall saying, "Come on, suck me off, I'm about to blow."

The mouth that had been blowing me moved off my cock and I heard him start sucking frantically on whoever was being pushy in the far stall, while I sat down on the john and slowly jacked my cock, using the spit from Mr. Center Stall for lube. The pushy guy came quick, since the guy in the middle could suck cock like a pro, having already demonstrated his talents to me, and the cum shot was nice and noisy and shook the steel walls—which I found really hot.

After blowing his load the guy in the far stall zipped up and left and the guy in the middle stall pressed his open mouth right up to the hole in our partition so I could see he was ready for me again. I obliged him by jamming my cock as far into his mouth and down his throat as I could and proceeded to pound away at his mouth pressed up to the hole for all I was worth. I was holding the top of the stall partition and using it for leverage and at one point I was slamming against the stall and his mouth so hard that I thought the partition might break away from the wall. The force of the pounding was causing his head and face to snap back from the hole an inch or two every time I slammed forward against the partition, and that really turned me on and made me fuck his mouth even harder.

Soon enough I could tell he was getting ready to cum, because he was making kind of strangling sounds around my dick. I picked up the pace and as he started to shoot I looked down and could see his knees resting on the floor under the partition below my cock and between my feet, as well as his big fat uncut cock, which was shooting all over my sneakers. Seeing that drove me over the edge and I slammed against the partition and his mouth one or two more times and then came so hard that I was rewarded with the very satisfying sound of choking coming from the throat in the next stall.

After shooting I sat back down on the toilet to get my breath and could hear the guy pulling his pants up next to me. As his stall door opened he said, "Thanks, guy." And left.

Having just had my first glory hole experience, I was not even close to being ready to go back to studying, so as soon as I zipped up I moved into the center stall, sat down on the toilet, and pulled my cock out to wait for whoever showed up next.

As Rick had said earlier in his description of the glory hole, it was "fairly active" to say the least, and I didn't have long to wait before some more contestants came in to check things out.

Scott

Wednesday Sept. 6, 2006: A Post From The Joint
Dear Scott,

I can't believe I ran out of phone minutes and can't call you to tell you what just happened. I guess I'll have to sit down with my little pencil nub and write it out for you, although that's not nearly as good as being able to hear your reaction.

Anyway, we've got this guy here I'll call Ricky Lee and he looks just like that guy, what's his name? You know, the hot young actor with the first and last names of female actresses, ohhhhh—Channing Tatum!!—but with lots and lots of really hot neo-Nazi and Aryan Nation tattoos. I've been really sweet to him, chatting him up all the time out on the track and buying him granola bars, since he's as broke as a person can be in prison, which is really fucking broke. He knows that I'm a huge homo and even though he's got a past that would make The Grand Kleagle of the Klu Klux Klan envious he's taken a shining to me and flirts outrageously all the time! So about five minutes ago he comes strolling into my cell/cube, obviously straight from the shower, since he's wrapped in a prison-issue towel and wearing his shower shoes and is still kind of glisteny with water, and he leans against my partition wall and I'm trying not to stare at his bulge (but not trying too hard) and I said, "Nice shower?"

Whereupon he replied, "Yeah. I jerked off and shot a big load." Said with a mischievous grin. And I said, "Sorry I missed it." Really flustered and turning red. And he said, "I've got some left."

And proceeded to reach under his towel and pull out his soft fat dick, which he squeezed until a long rope of cum drooled out and plopped on the floor of my cell! Then he smiled and winked and strolled out, and now I think I'm going to have a heart attack. Do you think that this means Ricky Lee and I are dating now?

Love ya,

Bill

DISASTER RELIEF

Greg Herren

"Most of the damage is upstairs," I said as I unlocked the front door to my apartment and pushed it open. I stood in the doorway and allowed him to pass. "Although we did get some mold down here on the walls." I shrugged. I'd shown the wreckage that had been my home for just two months to so many people by this time that it didn't affect me anymore. The first time I'd walked in after Katrina had gone through I had been in shock. You never expect to see your home in that condition; mold running down the walls, plaster wreckage covering the stairs, your bed a mildew factory. It had made me sick to my stomach.

Well, that and the smell coming from the refrigerator.

It was my home, it was the same apartment

I'd been so excited to move into a million years ago in June, but I didn't feel the same way about it as I did before.

Christian Evans, my FEMA inspector, whistled as he walked in and took a look around. "Nice place."

"It was." I used to love the high ceilings, the two ceiling fans, the curved staircase leading up to the second floor, and the hardwood floor I polished until it was like a mirror. Now the floor was covered with dust from the collapsed ceiling upstairs. The plaster on the walls in the living room was cracked, and the true enemy was evident on the ceiling—those horrible black spreading spots of mold that looked like inkblots. But at least the ever-present stench of mold and mildew was hardly noticeable anymore.

And I'd won my epic battle with the refrigerator.

"But I imagine you've seen a lot worse," I went on, hugging myself. It was a cool morning with a strong breeze blowing that made it seem colder, and of course I didn't have the heat turned on. Not much point in trying to warm the place when there was no ceiling upstairs. *Of course he's seen worse*, I scolded myself. That had been my litany ever since I'd come back.

You're one of the lucky ones, remember that.

Christian shrugged. He was a small man, maybe about five eight, in his early thirties. He was cute in that nondescript metrosexual "is he gay or straight?" way. He had a light brown goatee, and had gelled his brown hair into that just-got-out-of-bed look that seemed to be all the rage. Before the storm, I'd always referred to that style as the freshly fucked look. I'd never really cared for it much, but it worked on him. He had a way of grinning that somehow worked with the gelled hair. "I've been out to the Ninth Ward and Lakeview," he said as he pulled his laser pointer out of his pocket and started measuring the dimensions of the room. "So you lost your couch?"

"Mold. And the reclining chair, the coffee table." I sighed. I'd gone over the inventory of the losses so many times already I could say it all by rote. Our new couch, gone. The comfy old reclining chair I'd inherited from my workout partner who'd inherited it from a good friend who'd died. I loved that chair, used to sit in it all the time, thinking and writing in my head. "I was lucky, though, I know." Even knowing it to be true didn't make saying it feel any less hollow. I hadn't lost everything, like so many people I knew. Houses destroyed, mementoes and everything inside gone forever. So many of my friends were now homeless, sleeping on couches belonging to friends or relatives, living in campers, waiting for FEMA trailers while they tried to figure out what they were going to do about what used to be their homes. No, I had a place to live, and my source of income was still intact. I was able to come back to the city I loved, struggle to reestablish my life to some semblance of what it had been before. So many couldn't come back. So many others wouldn't. "But the kitchen is okay; I didn't lose anything in there except food."

He made some entries on his laptop. "I'll put you down for everything in the living room. What about television, VCR, that kind of thing?"

"Those are all okay." I shook my head. "It was weird how some things survived and some things didn't. I mean, the towel I hung up after my shower that morning, which was wet, didn't get moldy at all. It was stiff, but all I had to do was wash it and it was fine." I cut myself off, recognizing the post-Katrina babble coming on. If I didn't stop myself, I was going to list every single item I owned and what happened to it. And he was only interested in what I lost.

But how do you explain to someone that you've lost your soul? The inner core of your being?

You can't.

He shrugged out of his brown sport coat. He was wearing a white dress shirt underneath, tucked into a tight pair of boot cut jeans—and snakeskin cowboy boots. He placed the jacket on a wicker chair and I got a glimpse of his ass, which was round and hard. Definitely a nice ass. Before I would have stared at it, trying not to let drool dribble out of my mouth. I might have even tried to be flirtatious. He *might* be gay, after all. He turned back to me. "So let's see the upstairs."

I took a deep breath and started up the stairs. The upstairs still kind of bothered me, even though I'd seen it plenty of times. The ceiling was gone in the bedroom, hallway and bathroom. After the turn in the stairs, the walls were gone, ripped out by the handyman hired to repair the place. It was still a shock to see the bare beams, the debris I hadn't cleaned off the stairs, and the moldy carpet in the hallway. "It looks a lot better," I said as I went around the turn. "I cleaned out a lot of the debris already." I had. The stairs had been buried in dust and plaster at least two inches deep—as had the hallway and the bedroom. But I hadn't gotten everything up, and I could feel bits of plaster crunching underneath my shoes. The bathroom ceiling was still there, if covered in mold. But the patio door off the bathroom had been blown off its hinges by the wind, and the linoleum on the floor was peeling up.

Yet somehow my towels—and my wet one, at that—hadn't gotten moldy.

Christian whistled as we walked into the bedroom and looked up at the bare beams. You could see clear up to the outer roof, which had just been finished a few days earlier. He pulled out his laser pointer, and started measuring again, typing things into the laptop at a furious pace. "Bedroom set?"

"Gone."

"Any electronics?"

"Computer, scanner, printer, TV, DVD player."

He walked across to the bathroom and stuck his head in, then started typing again. "I'm putting you down for all toiletries, towels; all the bathroom stuff."

"Thanks." I started to correct him—the towels were okay—but stopped myself. Did it matter? I leaned against the wall and closed my eyes.

I could hear him typing away. Then he stopped. "Do you mind if I smoke?"

I opened my eyes. I laughed. "I think smoke is the least of my concerns at this point. Besides, I smoke—*smoked*—in the house. Before."

"Oh, thanks man." He shook a cigarette out of a crumpled pack of Pall Malls. "You laugh, but you'd be surprised. I was walking some woman through her house in Lakeview—total loss, it's going to have to be completely gutted and rebuilt—and she acted like I'd asked her to take poison or something when I asked if I could smoke, you know? I mean, what the hell difference did it make? The house was *ruined*. But she said no." He shrugged.

"That's crazy." I laughed. "Besides, I would think people would be nice to you." I went on, adding to myself, *since you control how much money they get to rebuild their lives.*

I was planning on being very nice.

"Tell that to them." He took a deep drag and looked around for an ashtray.

"Just use the floor."

He grimaced, then slid one of the windows open and flicked the ash outside. He gave me a little grin. "I just can't bring myself to do that."

"Habit, I guess—like the woman in Lakeview."

"Yeah." He leaned against the wall. "No, people aren't nice to us. They haven't forgotten the days after, you know, when we dropped the ball and the whole world was watching." He shook his head. "Of course, all of us didn't work for FEMA then, you know. We were hired as temps to help out with this mess...but they need someone to blame, I guess, and we're handy." He gave me a look. "I mean, you filed your claim two months ago and haven't seen a dime yet, right?" He shrugged. "That pisses people off—especially when other people have already gotten money. But the higher-ups keep changing everything from week to week."

"Yeah, well, being an asshole to you's not gonna make anything different, you know?" I'd raged myself against FEMA any number of times in the days since the storm, as I watched New Orleans die on television. "I appreciate you being so cool."

"Yeah." He opened his mouth to say something, then shut it.

"I'll just be glad when this is all over," I said, covering my face in my hands, "but I know it's never going to be, is it?"

"Hey." He stepped closer to me, and took my hands away from my face. "It's going to be okay."

I looked at his face. *Damn, he's cute,* I thought to myself, and the look on his face, the mix of concern and sympathy, despite everything he'd already seen, touched me deep into my soul. Without stopping to think, I bent my head down and brushed my lips against his.

He stepped back. "Um—"

"Sorry." I shrugged, holding up both hands.

A small smile crept over his face. "I was just wondering if you had a condom?"

I paused for a minute, and a slow smile spread over my face. *In here,* I thought, *not in the carriage house. Oh no, here in the apartment, that would be perfect, just perfect, besides all I have at the carriage house is an air mattress on the floor anyway.* I gave a little laugh. "Wait here."

I ran down the stairs without waiting for a response, out the front door and over to the carriage house. I grabbed my backpack, shoving a handful of condoms, lube and poppers into the front pouch, then slung it over my shoulder and went back out the door. As I walked back along the flagstones, I couldn't believe this was happening. *My FEMA inspector? Who would believe this?*

I wasn't sure I did myself.

When I got back up to my bedroom, he was leaning against the wall, smoking a cigarette. He had unbuttoned his shirt, and it fell open to reveal a hairy but lean torso. Black hair curled around his hard pecs, down a trail to his navel, and then down into the just barely visible waistband of what appeared to be black Calvin Kleins. He gave me a hesitant little smile, then ground the cigarette out under his boot. He stepped forward and shrugged the shirt down off his shoulders, revealing a smooth expanse of freckled muscle. He tilted his head down to the left, then looked up at me with round brown eyes. He bit his lower lip.

I put down the backpack and pulled my sweatshirt over my head. I reached into the bag and pulled out the poppers and inhaled. I stepped toward him, handing him the bottle. He held it to his right nostril, then the left, then put the top back on and set it down.

The rush hit me, and all I wanted right then, more than anything, more than my life back, more than my apartment the way it was, was to feel his bare skin against mine, to grind my swelling crotch against his. I stepped forward and put my arms around him, his skin soft yet firm to the touch, smooth and satiny, and I pressed my lips to the base of his throat, and I felt him start to growl as he thrust his pelvis forward against mine, and I began licking his throat.

"Oh my god," he whispered, his hands cupping my ass and squeezing, pulling me forward against him. "That feels so good, please don't stop, my god..."

As if I could.

He tasted slightly of sweat and maybe of soap. My tongue darted out, licking the top of his breastbone and then the hollow just above the bone. He moaned, shifting his weight from side to side, our crotches pressed against each other. I could feel his erection against mine, and I moved my hips just a bit to create some friction. I brought my hands up to his nipples and started flicking them slightly, enough to make them harden beneath my fingertips.

He pushed my head away from his neck and took a deep breath. "My god, dude."

I gave him a lazy smile and undid his belt with one hand while pinching his left nipple. Then I pulled the zipper down, slid my hand underneath his balls, and squeezed gently. "You like that, boy?"

"Oh, yes, sir," he breathed.

I slid the pants down to his ankles. He was wearing black Calvin Klein boxer-briefs that clung to his body. The head of his cock was poking out the top of the waistband. I licked my fingers and ran them over the tip. He shivered and twisted his head from side to side. I brought my lips to his throat again, and he gasped, a sound that I took to be pleasure. I ran my tongue down his torso, from the neck to the pecs—stopping there to suck on each nipple for a moment—and then to just below his navel. I pulled the underwear down, freeing his thick dick before enveloping it with my lips, my tongue twirling around the underside of it.

I slid one hand between his legs and began stroking the lower crack of his ass. He shook and trembled again, giving me the incentive to slip a probing finger in between the hard glutes. I felt hair, and was glad he wasn't one of those boys who shaved their asses. There was just something *nasty* about a boy who didn't make himself antiseptic and hairless that made my dick's urgency to enter him even more frantic and necessary.

I leaned away from him and smiled. He gave me a weak, almost limp smile between gasps for breath. I grabbed hold of his hips and spun him around and looked at the muscular white ass. Sure enough, there were black hairs inside its crack, and I spread his asscheeks with my hands and stuck my face in between, smelling him, darting my tongue out and licking at his hole. He arched his back, shoving his ass back into my face, and leaned forward, all of his weight resting on his forearms against the wall.

As I licked and probed his ass with my tongue, I felt my own need. It had been sublimated since the day I left with the cat and everything I could think to grab in my car. I hadn't thought about sex, about getting laid, hell, even about masturbating in the weeks that followed, as I watched the city die on national television, as I worried about my home and if I would ever be able to come back.

It felt somehow so right to eat his ass, as though I was

becoming myself again in a way I had forgotten.

I slid the condom over my cock and lubed it up, then massaged lube into his hole and slipped a finger inside. He let out another moan, and I smiled. He was ready, and so was I.

I slid the head of my cock into him, and his entire body stiffened. He rose up on his toes as a loud gasp was forced out of his throat, and a hand reflexively grabbed my left hip. "Easy," he whispered hoarsely. "It's big, oh god, it's big and I want it, but please go slow."

And even though I wanted to plunge it in, hard and brutal, ripping him apart and shoving him into the wall, I did as he asked, and went slowly, bit by bit, waiting with each further insertion until he relaxed. I leaned forward as I slid inside, kissing the back of his neck as my hands gripped his hips. Finally, he let go with a sigh and I slid the rest of the way in.

I didn't move. I just stood there, my cock deep inside of his body, and closed my eyes, tilting my head back.

This was life, breathing again. This was connecting with another human being for the first time in weeks, and the warmth of his body felt so right....

And I started moving, sliding back and forth slowly, listening to him moan, feeling him shivering and trembling with the pleasure my cock was giving him, and then his own need took control, and he began sliding himself back as I entered, until we were moving in a faster, more brutal rhythm.

His arms slapped against the wall.

"Yes," he repeated over and over again, breathing it out each time I pounded into him, louder and louder, his muscles flexing involuntarily, and I rode him, feeling my orgasm coming closer and closer. I started pounding harder, pulling him back toward me and slamming forward so hard that he was rising up on his toes as I tried to shove my entire body inside of him; I wanted to go deeper into him than any man ever had before, deeper than I'd ever gone before, wanted to reach the very core of his being, to touch his soul.

And then my mind exploded with the animalistic ecstasy of my orgasm, my entire body stiffening and my own breath exploding out of me, black spots dancing before my eyes because I couldn't catch my breath, and I had lifted him off the ground, impaling him, and he was shaking with me.

And then my breathing slowed.

I set him back down.

I slid out of him.

"Jesus," he whispered, turning around, a string of cum hanging from the head of his cock. He reached over and touched my face. "That was so intense...my god."

I smiled, unable to speak.

"Can I clean up at your place?" He gave me a weak smile. "I can't make my next appointment like this." He gestured at his sweat-soaked torso, and I noticed the cum spots on the wall. He followed my gaze, and grinned sheepishly. "Um, I had already put down replacing the walls in here."

I touched his lips with the forefinger of my right hand. "Thank you, Christian."

He lowered his head. "Thank you."

We walked back to the carriage house. I gave him a towel and went downstairs, lighting a cigarette and sitting on the front stoop. I heard the shower water running.

I smiled.

You're going to make it, I said to myself. *You're going to be just fine.*

I felt normal again.

THERE'S MORE TO KINK THAN LEATHER

Cat Tailor

Once again, it was a Saturday night, and Jason was in full leathers on his way to the Hole. Its patrons called it various things, depending on their moods: the Suck Hole, the Fuck Hole, the Hell Hole, the Sphincter, or just "the bar," as in, "Will you be at the bar tonight?"

"Yeah, you?"

"Yeah."

Whatever you called it, it was a playground for kinky faggots, and Jason was there a lot. There was a generic replacement for "Jason," too. Mostly they called him Sir.

Jason wondered who he'd beat tonight, and was slightly bored at the thought. Well, perhaps he'd shake things up and bottom to someone, then. He snickered. It wasn't that the idea of him bottoming was funny—he was more than willing to go there on occasion. It was funny to try and picture any of the Hole's regular denizens working up the nerve to approach him as a dom.

They were prudently respectful. Even the new ones. Jason could see the discreet pointing as old hands filled in fresh meat on which tops to approach only with extreme caution and signed waivers.

It slowly dawned on Jason that he wasn't walking anymore. He'd ambled to a stop in the middle of the sidewalk, city foot traffic diverting itself around him. Perhaps he wasn't in the mood?

He told himself he'd *get* in the mood. Sure, all he had to do was go there, and one or several eager bottoms would approach, and he'd beat the crap out of them until they begged to suck his cock. Or they'd suck his cock until they begged him to beat the crap out of them.

Sigh.

Not quite sure where he was going, Jason took a right instead of a left at the next corner. Then he wandered for a while, waiting for inspiration to strike. Soon enough, it did, in the form of a lean, young, extremely pretty boy lounging outside a bar. The sign read SUGAR'S, and if this sweet thing was advertising, he was doing a fine job. Jason pictured him on his knees, naked, tear tracks on his cheeks, and suddenly found his interest in his sexual life returning.

He entered the bar through, of all things, red velvet curtains. Inside he found a dim, smoky place. It was decorated in Early Drag Queen, with chaise lounges, zebra-print pillows, heavy crystal ashtrays, and—to complete the décor—numerous drag queens.

Oh shit, he'd found their secret lair.

Now, it wasn't that Jason had anything against gay men dressed up as women—to the contrary, he thought they gave the Pride Parade that special something it would otherwise lack. The particular blend of high camp and cattiness never seemed to get stale. And the lengths they went to in putting themselves together—it was impressive, even to a man who had leather tailor-made for his body. But he didn't sleep with them, and despite his air of ennui, he was looking to get laid tonight.

Turning around, Jason was halfway back to the curtains when a tall brunette slid in front of him. Glancing down, Jason saw that she was tall due to six-inch platforms—probably a little on the small side without. Pretty, pretty girl, too. Must be a gorgeous boy. Oh well, back to the bar.

Only she put out a hand, pressing her red talons against his leather vest.

"Where you goin' in such a hurry, Daddy? I think you out of your *juris-dick-shun*." The Puerto Rican lilt of her speech softened her words, and it took him a moment to process that she'd stopped him to make fun of him. For cowardice, no less.

Interesting.

"Yes, well, I figured that out myself, actually. I'll just be leaving you ladies to enjoy your evening."

She pouted, pushing out a full lower lip, shining with lacquer. "Oh, no, Daddy, surely you don't mean to leave us girls here alone, do you? Is been so long since we had any *entertainment*." She was pitching her words to carry, and laughter echoed from the nearest tables.

Jason sensed someone behind him, too close, and jumped like a bullwhip had cracked in Macy's. More laughter. He tried to see who it was, but found that the Puerto Rican queen in front of him had grabbed his face with her claws. "No, look at me, Daddy. Don't you worry about her. She's none of your business now."

Jason was pretty sure she was his business, whoever it was. She was right up behind him, pressing herself against his back. Long hair was brushing the skin above his vest. He could feel her hot breath on the side of his neck, and then she planted a feather-soft kiss in that perfect sweet spot.

He couldn't help it. He melted, just a little. His body shifted, his ass tilting up. When it did, he found it connecting with something he *was* familiar with—a nice hard cock, wrapped tight in fabric, pressing itself against him and straining to get free of its bonds.

He thought they packed their candy away, like back between their thighs. Was this the boy, then? No, he'd had short hair. Someone he hadn't seen in the back of the bar? Perhaps, but as he slid his hands back to gather information, he found a skirt, not pants.

Then his hand was slapped, and he pulled it back. A mocking voice from behind said, "Getting fresh already, are you? Who said you could touch Jezebel?"

Jason said, "Who said you could touch me?" That was better. It was time to regain control, and get the hell out of here before this turned into Hotel California.

He was looking into mock mournful eyes, as she shook her head in front of him. "Oh, no, Daddy, you come into our place. We know better than to walk into your place. You think because you wear all that nasty cow and make other men cry that makes you tough? You think because you look like Biker-Gets-a-Makeover that we all goin' to cringe and bow? Think again, papi."

Behind him, Jezebel's hands were busy. They were running up his thighs, squeezing his biceps. Pressed up against him, she started working her thigh between his chap-clad legs. Then her hand snaked around to the front, grabbing his package with the familiarity of an old lover.

"Maria, this Daddy's hard. Feel this shit!"

Oh, crap. He was, too. What did that mean? He was secretly yearning to be talked back to by mouthy drag queens? Or was he hoping to get some from these ladies in their clouds of perfume, their big hair and long nails? He was going to need therapy, definitely.

Maria took the invitation, and Jason looked down to see ten long, graceful arches of shining red stroking the front of his jeans.

He wasn't into men who look like women. So why did his dick just jump?

Jezebel left off fondling his cock and ran her hands down his arms. She gently wrapped her hands around his wrists, and pulled them back behind him. For some reason, it didn't occur to him to resist. When she wrapped a length of cloth—a scarf?—around them, again he didn't resist. When she pulled a knot tight, it occurred to him that perhaps he was being incredibly stupid.

"Okay, ladies, you've had your fun. I'll just be going back to my world now." He pulled to free his hands, and found that the knots didn't give. He pulled harder. No luck. Jason heard a distinctly nervous laugh come out of his throat. "Um, yeah, okay, could you untie me, please? I really do want to go." Well, he could always just make a break for it, and get untied by a passerby on the street.

Only they had company. Looking around, Jason saw that

where there had been just two girls, now there were five or six. He was actually surrounded. Scanning their faces, he wondered how he'd ever dismissed drag queens as frivolous creatures before. They looked like a wolf pack. They glittered, but then, so do fangs. And knives.

"Honey, you're not going anywhere. We're tired of giving each other hand jobs in the bathroom between bumps."

"Way too much of Mama's home cooking. Time for a little spicy takeout."

They were moving in closer, all of them near enough to bite. If he was feeling like having his eyes scratched out and his teeth removed with eyelash curlers, that is. Hands were all over him. Was he really pushing his hips forward, trying to get a little firmer pressure from the delicate touches on his cock?

"What do you think of this ass, girls?"

More hands. Some of them got more invasive, pushing his asscheeks apart and running along the seam. "I think it's good. Good enough, anyway."

"Yeah, but chaps can be deceptive. If they're well made, they can work like a push-up bra, showing off a bit more than you got."

"Sing it sister!"

"Let's find out what he's made of!"

One pair of hands held on to his wrists behind, hiking them up enough to make him groan. Another pair, Maria's soft hands, wrapped around his throat, tight enough to restrict his air. "Don't move, papi. We want to see your meat, and you gonna give it to us, right?"

Three or so pairs of hands stripped off his chaps and yanked down his jeans, in about five seconds. Jason realized he was standing in the middle of a bar with his pants down around his boots. His dick was waving in the breeze, betraying him to these harpies.

"Whatchoo think, ladies? I can't see from here!"

"Oh, Maria, it *is* a good ass. Now you tell me, what's the meat report?"

"Grade-A U.S. Choice Prime USDA someshit like that." They giggled. "Curve to the left, nice ridge, fat head. A tonsiltickler, if you were one of his little slave boys and had to suck on that thing."

Jason felt he ought to say *something*. "You don't have to be my slave boy to suck me. I'd let you, for example."

"Ha! Oh, you're a funny Daddy. Are we going to suck his cock, girls?"

"No!"

"Hell no!"

"What *are* we going to do with his cock?"

"We're going to decorate it!"

From nowhere, they produced accessories. In moments, he had a stack of bracelets on his dick, jangling as he breathed. "Don't let them fall off, Daddy. We'll be very upset if you don't properly appreciate our gifts." Someone worked a large hoop earring around the head of his cock. It fit snugly, making him aware of the blood in his dick with each beat of his heart. He looked on in disbelief as someone drew a little smiley face in red lipstick.

Finally, they produced yet another earring, this one with a long fall of gold chain, or beads, or both. His vision was blurring a little, he couldn't be sure.

"Maria, I think you need to ease up a little."

"Oh! Yeah, I forgot. I like hanging on to them by their throats."

"Yes, we know, dear. All part of why you need to get them to adjust your meds."

"*Claro que si*, but not tonight!"

The earring had a long arch of wire that held it in the ear. A platinum blonde was crouched down in front of him, methodically opening up the wire to a wider angle. She repeated the procedure with its mate. Then, she squeezed the top of his cock to open up his piss slit. She slid the wires in him, one after the other. The earrings dangled, light as air and yet so very *there*.

He was still hard. Fuck.

"Dance for us, papi. Shimmy and shake."

"Okay, look, you've had your little kidnapping and humiliation scene, here. Now, you know I'm not going to dance for you."

"We do?"

"Oh, really?"

The one who had been identified as Jezebel leaned around so he could see her face. She maintained her pressure on his hands, though. Bitch. Sexy, too. Pale skin, straight dark hair. Slightly narrow eyes outlined in garish shadow.

Shifting her grip to free up a hand, she produced a lipstick in his line of sight. "See this, Daddy? I'm now going to cram this up your ass."

With that, the struggle began. Jezebel held his hands up at a painful angle with one hand. Other girls held on to his arms, keeping him from moving far. Hands were trying to grab his asscheeks, to open him up for the lipstick's invasion.

Jason started trying to dodge the lipstick coming at him from behind. He felt the creamy stick slide across his ass, and he'd jump.

This went on for a while. Slowly, he realized there were a

few girls in front of him, just watching and clapping. Then he realized he'd been dancing for them, making the jangling things shake for their amusement. He'd been well and truly trapped—he could make an open mockery of himself by performing, or he could make an open mockery of himself by being sodomized by that little tube of paint.

For a dizzy moment, he realized he was outclassed. These girls could teach him a thing or two about sadism.

He must have stilled with his epiphany, because he felt the cool pressure of the lipstick finding the hole it sought. He jumped, trying to get away, but Jezebel had found her mark and went with him. She pushed, and it went in. Despite all the messages screaming in his brain, something in Jason reacted the way it always did to an anal invasion.

He opened up, and his dick sprang higher, arching toward his belly.

"That's it, Daddy. You give that ass to me, darling. I'll make good use of it, I promise." The cool metal of the tube was gone, and instead, a gloved finger was entering him. Jason kept waiting for a sharp edge, but he didn't feel any. How was that possible? They all had fingernails like creatures man tries to render extinct.

Well, however she did it, oh, it was a nice finger. He could feel it pressing itself around all sides of his asshole, just inside. There was a heavy feeling, something thicker than lube. Was there lipstick up inside him? What was she doing?

He didn't follow the quick conversation happening behind him, and then a cell phone was held out in front of him. "Look! It's your asshole, all covered with lipstick. Now, with a sweet little bull's-eye pucker like that, how can we resist your invitation?"

Jason moaned and closed his eyes. It might take him years to get that image out of his mind. And they were going to have it forever, sending it to each other, pulling it out on party nights as proof of what they did to the leather Daddy who wandered onto their turf alone. *Just don't tell them your name,* he thought.

"I want to send that to Candy—she's got to get down here!"

"Let's tell her who it is, too. Her roommate goes to that leather bar sometimes, he might know this guy."

Jason thought he'd cry as they rummaged through his pants, finding his wallet, and then learning his name. "Tell her it's Jason Stockton. See if her roommate knows him."

Jason found himself begging. "Please, please, don't do that. That's my world, my life. Yes, he'll know me, everyone knows me there. Please, it's a small community—people would know no matter where I went. Oh, please, I'm not done being a topman."

Laughter. "You don't look like much of a topman right now, do you, Daddy?"

"No, ladies, I don't. Please, I'll do whatever you want. I'm begging you."

Maria giggled. "Papi, you're going to do whatever we want anyway! We already got you to dance your little pee-pee for us, and we fucked you with a tube of pretty paint, and we have photographic evidence. You think we're not going to fuck you, too?"

Jason hung his head. He felt a tear slowly make its way down his cheek. Was this how his bottoms felt when he gave them impossible problems to solve and then mocked their inability to think clearly?

Then inspiration came to him. Really fucked-up inspiration.

Oh, wow. And he was really going to say it, wasn't he?

Yes. He was. "Please, I'll do whatever you want again. I'll come back next month."

He could feel the delight, as if they'd sheathed their claws for a second and started purring. "Yes, that's a nice idea. Only you come back every month. Forever."

"And as soon as you miss one, we send out the picture."

"Well, yeah, along with the other picture."

"What other picture?"

"The one we're about to take, of him bent over a table with Jezebel's candy up his ass!"

Jason felt a second tear trail down his face. His dick was still hard.

Laughing, the girls dragged him over to the nearest rickety bar table. They pushed him over it, having to pull his dick away from his body to stick it under the table. "So you don't scuff my pretty earrings, darling." The bracelets fell to the floor with a tinkling clatter. His head hung over the far side, which was just as well. He didn't want to see anything or anyone, ever again.

Jezebel walked around in front of him and slapped his face. "Lift up your head, Daddy. I want you to see what you're getting into."

She hiked up a short red skirt, showing stocking tops, garters, and black lacy panties. Her cock wasn't terribly long, but it was nice and thick. He could see its outline clearly through the shiny fabric, and his mouth watered.

Stroking it a couple of times, Jezebel grinned at him. "You're still having a good time, aren't you? Sick fucking bastard." Then she pulled it out. "Here, get it good and wet. It's for your own good."

"Such a cliché, but still so true."

As she stepped up to his face, Jason couldn't believe the smell of it. It was soft and girlish, a sweet powdery smell. And then there was the ripe musk of a man, the heady scent coming off her balls, the glistening drop of pre-come oozing from the slit. His head had no idea to do with this contradictory input.

His mouth did. It opened wide, his tongue reaching to wrap around the head and stroke it. He slurped it in, pulling with his lips to try to get it further into his mouth. Jezebel obliged, moving closer to him. He was fully plugged, balls up against his chin, sucking and licking the thing like it was his only salvation. Finally, something he could hang on to. He knew dick. Definitely.

All too soon, she pulled out, his spit trailing after her, connecting her dick to his mouth. After she'd walked out of his line of sight, it was only seconds before he felt hands on his asscheeks, opening him wide. The feeling of cool wetness from his spit was quickly superseded by the hot flesh that followed. Jason felt a wave of hot shame, remembering the bull's-eye she was hitting.

Not that it mattered as she sank inside her target. Jason arched his back, wanting to fight against the startling girth entering him, and at the same time trying to relax. He wasn't fucked often enough for it to be easy.

Bless her wicked heart, once Jezebel was all the way in, she stopped. She stayed there, breathing with him, allowing him to catch up to the size of her. His must not be the first tight ass she'd fucked.

Before he was quite ready, she started moving again. Stroking in and out, she started talking to him. "That's right,

Daddy, you like it like this, don't you? Your ass is ours, now, forever. We're gonna do you like this, one after another, every single fucking month until you get too dried up for us to want to touch. And then we'll bend you over our walkers and fuck you with our canes, because we're that kind of vindictive bitches and we *own* you. Yeah, we own this tight ass, and that willing mouth, and your fucking leather pride, and all the rest of your safe little world."

"Speaking of mouth, I want me some-a that."

Glittery high-heeled platform boots appeared in Jason's view. Yeah, she probably did. He was spared the effort of lifting his head when she just yanked him up by the back of his vest. Before he could even find out what color her panties were, she had speared his mouth with an impressively long, uncut cock.

Heaven, or hell? Such a fine line.

Whichever it was, he went to work. Best not to disappoint his blackmailers. He knew they'd have many photos, on several phones, of Jezebel plowing him. They'd make sure to get his face. They were smart, and cruel.

And kind. The cock in his mouth was delicious, battering the back of his throat like he battered his boys. He was crying and choking, his mucous helping him while reminding him of his helplessness. His ass was on fire, lipstick and spit not making the best possible lubricant for a serious reaming.

Despite all of it, he was rock hard, and he moaned and thrashed when graceful fingers and long nails reached under the table and started jacking him off. The hoop around the head of his cock got even tighter. He couldn't feel the gold earrings anymore and the small part of his mind that was still observing things wondered if they'd fallen off.

Jezebel was still going slow and steady, but the cock in

his mouth was speeding up. Wanting to be helpful, he sucked harder, increasing the pressure like he preferred when he was about to come. Completely cutting off his air, the dick rammed down his throat, shooting a load of hot come deep inside him.

Oh, god, he was being used like a party favor. In seconds, there was another dick in his face. He sucked it, just trying to please. The hand had left his cock long before he came, which was just as well. He couldn't imagine accommodating Jezebel after orgasm.

Jezebel sped up, thrusting harder, grinding Jason's hips against the rough wooden table. He was moaning in time, trying to breathe around the dick down his throat.

In desperation, trying to get it to end, Jason clamped his ass tight around Jezebel's cock. Holding on as tight as he could, he wasn't surprised when Jezebel rammed herself deep in him one last time. Her cry was high and feminine; her dick twitching in his ass, all man.

She finally softened and slipped out, and someone else slid in. Great, at least Jezebel's load would provide the sloppy seconds with some lubrication. It was so good, so terribly good. How many of them were there? How many would use him before the night was over?

It was more than a couple. Jason felt buried in bangles, covered in perfume and jizz. They had shot in his hair, and come was running down the crack of his ass. Maria had whispered as she slid up inside him, "That's right, papacita, perracita, little hungry bitch puta, yeah, let Maria get what she wants. Good papi. Oh, yeah."

Someone untied his wrists partway through, and he still didn't try to get away. Instead he clutched the sides of the table. Then he reached out and found he didn't get slapped away when he held on to the ass of the girl fucking his mouth.

When he pulled her toward him, driving her deeper down his throat than she'd been reaching on her own, she gave a high groan and came, her dick jerking in his mouth. Oh yeah—a little control.

Not that the feeling lasted.

It seemed they were all done using him, at least for the moment. Slowly, Jason lifted his head to look around. Their skirts were back in place. Aside from being a bit flushed, they all looked just as beautifully put together as they had when he'd walked in.

"Yeah, we look good, don't we, Daddy? You look like hammered crap."

"He looks like when I've used the last tissue to take off my lipstick, and then later I fish it out of the trash to wipe up my load."

"Precisely. But don't take our word for it."

Another cell phone was shoved in his face. There he was, leather vest, chaps around his ankles. One drag queen up his ass, another distending his cheeks with her meat. It was a good shot, nicely framed, clearly identifiable. Yup, they owned him.

"Come on, Jason Stockton, don't be so glum about it. Admit it, you had a good time."

"Not a *good time*, though—he's still hard!"

"Oh, well, that won't do." The speaker was another blonde, this one with black skin and legs for days. She stepped forward and pointed at her red vinyl stilettos. "Get up, bitch, and pay your tribute to these shoes. Just to, you know, seal our bargain."

"Um, what?" asked Jason.

"Beat off. Shoot your load on my shoes. Carefully—you hit my stockings and I'll get creative."

They hadn't been already? Shakily, Jason unstuck himself from the table. He managed to stand somehow.

Putting his hand on himself, he couldn't believe how aroused he was. He dropped to his knees so he'd be closer to his target. He only had to stroke himself a few times before he shot long ribbons of spunk all over those pretty, girly shoes.

He'd never look at women's feet the same way again.

Jason didn't have to be told what to do next. He bent forward and methodically licked every drop of cooling come off her shoes. When he started to move away, she tapped her toe impatiently.

"You know the drill, shithead."

Yes, he did. He cleaned up the floor as well. God, it was disgusting. He'd had no idea what he was putting people through.

"Well, ladies, do you think he's learned his lesson?"

"I don't think he's the same bored little Daddy he was when he came in here."

"Shall we kick him back out into the night?"

"Let's clean him up first, he looks an awful mess." Lord only knew where all the wet wipes came from, but in moments he'd been wiped off from stem to stern. Or something like that.

They replaced his clothing, their many hands making as quick work of replacement as removal. Maria held up a hand mirror. "Look, papi, you're all pretty again!"

He couldn't help it. He reached out and grabbed her, pulled that pouty Latin mouth toward him and kissed the hell out of her. The rest of them screeched and whistled in appreciation.

"Ooh, I think Maria's got her a little Daddy boyfriend!"

"I think you're right."

They were still chattering, a flock of dangerous geese, as he strode out into the night.

It still wasn't too late for the Hole. If he could find a way to explain the perfume, he could go straight there. Now that he'd had a little lesson in kink, it was probably time to pay it forward.

At the Hole, the boys sprang to attention for their Daddy, the drag queen's willing bitch.

Now *that* was kinky.

ABOUT THE AUTHORS

SHANE ALLISON is the author of five chapbooks of poetry, most recently *Black Fag* and *I Want to Fuck a Redneck*. His poems and short stories have been published in Velvet Mafia, Suspect Thoughts, Outsider Ink, juked, Softblow, *McSweeney's, I Do/I Don't: Queers on Marriage, Best Black Gay Erotica, Sexiest Soles, Cowboys: Gay Erotic Tales, Van Gogh's Ear, Chiron Review, Muscle Worshippers, Love in a Lockup*, zafusy, and *S.M.U.T.* His work is forthcoming in *Best Gay Love Stories: New York City* and *Sodom and Me: Queers on Fundamentalism*. He gets email at starsissy42@ hotmail.com.

JONATHAN ASCHE says: "I know it's more marketable to label my stories as 'erotica', but I'm more comfortable thinking of them as pornography, albeit good pornography." His short stories, be they erotica or porn, have appeared in *Playguy, Inches, Torso, Honcho, Men,* and *In Touch for Men,* and have been featured in the anthologies *Friction 3, Three the Hard Way, Manhandled, Buttmen 2* and *3, Best Gay Erotica 2004* and *2005,* and *Hot Gay Erotica.* He is also the author of the erotic novel *Mindjacker.* Asche lives in Atlanta with his husband, Tomé, and their neurotic pets.

DALE CHASE has been writing erotica for eight years, with more than one hundred stories published in various men's magazines and anthologies, including translation into German. Her first literary effort was published this year in the *Harrington Gay Men's Fiction Quarterly. The Company He Keeps,* her collection of Victorian gentlemen's erotica, is due in 2007. Chase lives near San Francisco and is at work on a collection of ghostly male erotica.

BOB CONDRON is the author of two gay erotic novels, *Easy Money* and *Sweating It Out,* and is editor of the anthologies *Daddy's Boyz* and *Working Stiff.*

WILLIAM MELOYD CULLUM was born and raised in Virginia but spent most of his adult life living in New York City, where he pursued a career as an artist. His work has been represented by Debs & Co. in New York, and he has exhibited at P.S.1 and in collected exhibitions at Lennon and Weinberg in New York and with the Visual Aids Foundation. He is currently serving a seven-year, three-month sentence in U.S. federal prison, a victim of America's failed war on drugs. For more information: http://billinexile.blogspot.com.

DRUB's images—proto-pornography for the punk and skate-board generation—are a new queer archetype with a subversive comic-book style, colorful manifestos of youthful lust. Mixing traditional fine art techniques with today's technology, his artwork perverts the mind and the medium; his distinctive images have previously been featured in *Blue*, *Freshmen*, *Gay-News Amsterdam* and *Instigator Magazine*, and exhibited in Amsterdam, Berlin, Toronto and the United States. Find him online at: www.drubskin.com.

GREG HERREN is the author of five critically acclaimed mystery novels, including *Mardi Gras Mambo*, and the editor of several anthologies, including *Love Bourbon Street: Reflections on New Orleans*. He has published numerous short stories and articles, and writes a monthly column on erotica writing for www.erotica-readers.com.

DALE LAZAROV is best known as the writer/editor of *Sticky*, an album of erotic stories of man-on-man carnality and sweetness produced in collaboration with illustrator Steve MacIsaac. Future volumes of *Sticky* with other collaborators, as well as a new series of gay erotic graphic novels, are scheduled for 2007 and beyond. Lazarov lives in Chicago.

BLAIR MASTBAUM's first novel, *Clay's Way*, won a Lambda Literary Award and was selected by the New York Public Library for its 2005 Books for the Teen Age list. He produced, shot, and acted in the 2005 Sundance Film Festival feature, *Ellie Parker*, directed by Scott Coffey. He lives in Brooklyn, New York, where he is working on his next novel, *Push*, and squandering time on his web journal, *Land of the Bat*. His website is www.blairmastbaum.com.

DAVID MAY first made his mark writing for *Drummer* and other gay skin magazines in the 1980s, and is the author of *Madrugada: A Cycle of Erotic Fictions*. His work has appeared in numerous magazines and anthologies, including *Mentsch*, *Kosher Meat*, *Flesh and the Word 3*, *Best of Best Gay Erotica 2* and *Hot Gay Erotica*. He lives in Seattle (where he is still working on that damn novel) with his husband and two cats.

JAY NEAL is a longtime connoisseur of beards and aficionado of guys with body hair. His favorite flavor in men is "husky," and those best described as "big lugs" are lovingly treated in his fiction, a vocation he was called to late last century. His stories have appeared in several magazines and more than a dozen anthologies. He and his partner share a life of domestic contentment in suburban Washington, D.C. For more: http://bearcastle.com/jayneal.

SCOTT D. POMFRET is coauthor of *Surf 'N' Turf*, the latest in the Romentics series of Harlequin-style romance novels for gay men. His short stories have been published in *Post Road*, *Genre Magazine*, *Fresh Men: New Gay Voices*, *Best Gay Love Stories 2005* and *2006*, *Best Gay Erotica 2005*, and many other magazines and anthologies. For more information, visit www.scottpomfret.com and www.romentics.com.

DOMINIC SANTI is a former technical editor turned rogue whose dirty stories have appeared in many dozens of anthologies and magazines, including *Best American Erotica*, *Best Gay Erotica*, *Freshmen: The Best* and *His Underwear*. Santi's latest solo book is the German collection *Kerle im Lustrausch* (*Horny Guys*). Forthcoming plans include more short stories, a heretical novel, and another trip to LaCrosse.

SIMON SHEPPARD is the author of *In Deep: Erotic Stories*; *Kinkorama*; *Sex Parties 101* and the award-winning *Hotter Than Hell*. He's also the editor of the forthcoming *Homosex: 60 Years of Gay Erotica*. This is his lucky thirteenth appearance in the *Best Gay Erotica* series, and his work also appears in about two hundred other anthologies, including several editions of *The Best American Erotica*. He writes the syndicated column "Sex Talk," lives queerly in San Francisco, and hangs out at www.simonsheppard.com. Every word of his story is true.

C. SCOTT SMITH is a displaced New Yorker living in the Pacific Northwest with his boyfriend Richard and their two dogs, Moby and Ripley. He attended Kenyon College and served in a combat infantry rifle company in the United States Marine Corps before moving to NYC and pursuing a career as a professional homosexual. He is working on a novel that may or may not include gratuitous and sleazy sex. Scott and Bill have been friends for more than twenty years. The material excerpted here is from the blog Bill in Exile, a collection of letters exchanged between Bill and Scott "while Bill is locked up in prison for selling methamphetamine to upper middle-class gay white boys in New York City." The full correspondence: http://billinexile.blogspot.com.

ALEX STRAND is a late twentysomething, horny, gay guy living in NYC. He loves men, muscles, sex, porn, and chocolate, and has a particular thing for "straight" guys; he likes to try on some different fetishes but is usually braver in his imagination than in his actions. "Hot Sales Guy" is an excerpt from his almost-daily blog, The Great Cock Hunt, which chronicles his quest for dick in NYC, lightly sprinkled with his attempts at being a boyfriend and finding a relationship. His adventures continue at www.thegreatcockhunt.com.

CAT TAILOR's work includes the BDSM novel *In the Spider's Web*, the adult game *The Pansexual Perverts' Play Pack*, the sex advice column "Chasing Your Tail? Ask Cat: Advice for Fuckers, Players, and Perverts" on shadesbeyondgray.com, and short stories that have appeared in *Hot Gay Erotica*, twobigmeanies.com, sexuality.org, shadesbeyondgray.com, *The Bottom Line*, Amoret Online and the 'zine *Problem Child*. She has been interviewed on Playboy Radio and "SexLife Live." Her website is www.CatTailor.com, email CatTailor@gmail.com.

ALANA NOEL VOTH has been reading Scott Heim, Bill Brent, Dennis Cooper, and Martin Hyatt lately, and has been inspired. She was equally inspired by Joseph Gordon-Levitt's performance in the film *Mysterious Skin*. Her story "Rock Stars in Particular Order" won third prize in a contest sponsored by Cleansheets, and her story "Genuflection" appeared in *Best Gay Erotica 2004* and *Best American Erotica 2005*. Her blog, *My Mom Writes Erotica*, is at http://alananoel.typepad.com/

ABOUT THE EDITORS

RICHARD LABONTÉ and his partner Asa live some of the time in a wee Perth, Ontario apartment, and some of the time in a sprawling ten-bedroom farmhouse on two hundred acres of land near Calabogie, Ontario, purchased thirty years ago with a bunch of straight college-era friends who still mostly like each other. From 1979 to 2000, he helped found and then manage A Different Light Bookstores in Los Angeles, New York, West Hollywood, and San Francisco. He has edited the *Best Gay Erotica* series since 1996; coedited *The Future is Queer* (Arsenal Pulp Press, 2006) with Lawrence Schimel; reviews one hundred books a year for Q Syndicate, which distributes his fortnightly column, "Book Marks"; writes the sort-of-monthly subscription newsletter *Books* to *Watch Out For/Gay Men's Edition*; writes book reviews for *Publishers Weekly*; and, to make a living, edits technical writing. Contact: tattyhill@gmail.com.

TIMOTHY J. LAMBERT was born and raised in rural Maine. Although he had a vivid imagination, he couldn't picture himself at college, much less hanging on the Quad with Biff and Skip. Instead, he lived in NYC for a decade, working an assortment of odd jobs—frozen-yogurt jockey, background characters onstage with the American Ballet Theater, shoe salesperson to the stars, and keyboardist and lyricist for a band, among others—gaining experiences to form into fodder for future works of fiction. He coauthored *Three Fortunes in One Cookie* and *The Deal* (both from Alyson books) with Becky Cochrane and, as one-fourth of Timothy James Beck, he coauthored *It Had To Be You*, *He's the One*, *I'm Your Man* and, most recently, *Someone Like You* (all from Kensington Books). His short story "The End of the Show" was published in Alyson's *Best Gay Love Stories 2005*, and Lambert and Cochrane are editing an anthology of romance stories for Haworth Press. He lives in Houston with his dog, Rexford G. Lambert. For more info: www.timothyjlambert.com.